MAY 3 0 2

W9-CTG-143

BULLETS AND LIES

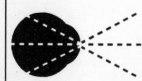

This Large Print Book carries the
Seal of Approval of N.A.V.H.

A TALBOT ROPER NOVEL

BULLETS AND LIES

ROBERT J. RANDISI

THORNDIKE PRESS

A part of Gale, Cengage Learning

GALE
CENGAGE Learning·

Detroit • New York • San Francisco • New Haven, Conn • Waterville, Maine • London

GALE
CENGAGE Learning·

Thorndike Press® Large Print Western.
The text of this Large Print edition is unabridged.
Other aspects of the book may vary from the original edition.
Set in 16 pt. Plantin.

LIBRARY OF CONGRESS CATALOGING-IN-PUBLICATION DATA

Randisi, Robert J.
  Bullets and lies : a Talbot Roper novel / by Robert J. Randisi. — Large print ed.
    p. cm. — (Thorndike Press large print Western)
  ISBN-13: 978-1-4104-5402-7 (hardcover)
  ISBN-10: 1-4104-5402-9 (hardcover)
  1. Retired military personnel—Fiction. 2. Medal of Honor—Fiction. 3. Large type books. I. Title.
PS3568.A53B85 2012
813'.54—dc23   2012035095

Published in 2012 by arrangement with The Berkley Publishing Group, a member of Penguin Group (USA) Inc.

Bullets and Lies

PROLOGUE

The heydays of Dodge City were long gone by the time Talbot Roper rode into town. When the Atchison, Topeka & Santa Fe Railroad came to Dodge in 1872, the town boomed. Many railroad cars a day filled with buffalo hides and meat left there, and just as many arrived carrying supplies. The streets — both Front Streets, one on each side of the railroad tracks — were lined with wagons and filled with people. But by 1880, when the Santa Fe railroad was completed, the good times were over and people started to leave. Now, almost six years later, the town was quiet, almost dead.

These days Roper was a private investigator working out of Denver. His job took him to big cities, ghost towns, and everything in between. And he adapted to his surroundings with equal comfort.

In Denver, New York, San Francisco, he wore a fancy suit with a matching hat, carried a short-barreled .32 in a shoulder rig, a derringer in his vest pocket, and a straight razor in his boot because it was more comfortable than a knife.

Out on the trail throughout the West, in towns or the Territories, he wore trail clothes and a worn Stetson, nothing that would make him stand out. He carried a Peacemaker in his holster, a second one in a holster affixed to the leather of his saddle with needle and heavy thread. The razor was still in his left boot, the derringer in his right, and a Winchester rifle in a scabbard on his saddle. He had a third Peacemaker in his saddlebag. No matter what environment he was in, he was ready for action.

He had proven himself many times over during his tenure with the Union during the Civil War. After acquitting himself well in a half-dozen battles, he had been recommended for transfer to the Union Intelligence Service to serve under Major E. A. Allan — otherwise known as Allan Pinkerton. There, working mostly undercover, he learned investigative techniques from Pinkerton, successfully rounding himself into a man of action and intelligence.

This case had started right there in his home city of Denver and had taken him across the plains to Dodge City, with a lot of bloodshed in between. It seemed fitting that it should end here, where the blood of legends had soaked into the soil many years ago, and still resided there.

Roper followed the trail he'd been tracking for miles right to the edge of Dodge City. There the trail mixed with others, but he was still able to make out a distinction he'd found in the right hind. The tracks led right into town and seemed fairly fresh.

Roper directed his horse to the livery, which was still where it had always been. He dismounted and collected his belongings before turning the animal over to the livery man. It had been so long since he'd been there — or had paid any attention to the goings-on in Dodge — that he did not know who was presently the law in town.

"Any strangers come to town in the past hour or so?" Roper asked the man.

"Not that I seen."

"Who's the law in Dodge these days?"

The livery man stroked the horse's damp neck as he said, "The sheriff is Pat Sughrue, the marshal is Bill Tilghman."

"Tilghman is here?" Roper asked.

"Yessir, been the marshal here for over two years," the man said.

"Well, that's good news," Roper said.

"You know the marshal?"

"I do, indeed. Thanks."

Roper carried his gear and went in search of a hotel. Most of the ones he remembered were gone, but when he came to the Dodge House, he was happy to see that it was still operating.

"I'd like a room," he said to the bored desk clerk.

"Take your pick," the clerk said. "We got plenty."

"Just one overlooking the street would be good."

"Take four," the clerk said, handing him the key. "Stay as long as you like."

Roper went to his room, dropped his saddlebags on the bed, leaned his rifle against the wall, and went to the window. In the old days the street would have been teeming with wagons and horses and people. On this day he saw a couple of small boys chasing a wagon wheel down the street and that was it.

He decided not to waste any time. He collected his rifle, left the room, and headed for the marshal's office.

Bill Tilghman looked up from his desk as the door to his office opened. He frowned, seeming confused for a moment, the way you are when you see someone someplace you don't expect to.

"As I live and shit, Talbot Roper," he said, "what the hell . . ."

"Bill," Roper said. "Busy?"

The marshal stood up, his hand outstretched, but did not come out from behind the desk. Roper noticed that the experienced lawman was wearing an empty holster. That was unlike him.

"It's good to see you," Tilghman said, pumping Roper's hand.

"You, too, Bill," Roper said, studying his friend's face closely.

The office had changed very little over the years. Just a desk, an extra chair and a stove, some file cabinets and gun racks. But it somehow felt different.

"What brings you to Dodge City?" Tilghman said, waving to the empty chair. "Coffee?"

"I could use a stiff drink," Roper said, "but coffee will do — for now."

Tilghman smiled and said, "I've got that."

He sat, opened a drawer, and pulled out a bottle of whiskey and two mugs. After pouring a generous dollop into each mug, he handed one to Roper.

"Thanks." The detective took a huge swallow. The heat warmed him. Tilghman

11

sipped, regarded Roper over the rim of his mug.

"That do the trick?" Tilghman asked.

"Oh, yeah."

The lawman sat back in his chair. He didn't look at all comfortable.

"What's goin' on, Roper?" he asked. "You're a long way from Denver. What brings you to a dead town like Dodge?"

"Dead?" Roper asked. "Is that the right word?"

"Oh, yeah," Tilghman said. "This town is long dead. Ain't no better word for it, believe me."

"Why are you still here, then?"

"I won't be for much longer," Tilghman said. "I'm headin' out in a month or so when my term is over. Bought me a little place."

"A ranch?"

"Yep. Gonna raise some horses."

"Where?"

"Near here," the marshal said. "What the hell are you doin' here? This ain't the kinda place to stop in for a visit."

"It's a long story," Roper said. "I started tracking a man from Denver, and I think he's here."

"What's his name?"

"Sender," Roper said. "John Sender."

12

"Should I know him?"

"I don't think so," Roper said. "Not yet anyway. Maybe not if I can catch him and cut his killing spree short."

"What's he look like?"

"Tall, broad shouldered, black hair, about forty," Roper said. "Wears a silver-plated Peacemaker, likes to use it."

"Far as I know, nobody like that's ridden into town," Tilghman said.

"His trail leads here."

"Could you have beat him here?"

Roper thought a moment, then said, "Could be. His trail led me this way, but I can't say he definitely rode in here."

"You huntin' bounty now, Roper?"

"Not exactly," he said. "I was hired by a man whose son was killed by Sender. They argued over a poker game, but everyone said it just looked like an excuse for Sender to gun the kid. I'm inclined to believe it, because he's killed three more men between there and here."

"What about the local law?"

"Once Sender left Denver, the police there didn't much care," Roper explained. "The boy's father isn't a politician, so nobody seemed to care except him."

"But he had enough money to hire you."

"He did," Roper said. "He somehow managed to pull it together."

"And you don't come cheap."

"No, but the best rarely do," Roper said. His eyes moved around the room. The rifle rack was full, cell block keys were hanging on a wall peg. The door to the cell blocks was open. The shutters of the front window were closed. He looked at Tilghman again. The man was staring at him intently.

Roper stood up. "Well, if you can't help me, I'll check with the sheriff and then have a look around town myself."

"Good idea," Tilghman said. "Pat Sughrue's a good man."

Roper walked to the door, and Tilghman remained behind his desk. He hadn't moved from that spot the entire time Roper was there, except to stand up. Roper remembered Tilghman as the kind of man who was normally in motion. And while he looked restless, he hadn't taken steps to remedy the situation. He just . . . sat.

"Stop back in before you leave, Roper."

"I'll do that, Bill."

He stepped out and closed the door behind him.

Roper worked his way around to the back of the marshal's office. He knew something was wrong, but since the shutters were

14

closed, he had no view from the front window. His only chance was to try to get in through the back door.

Before reaching the back, he came to a high barred window and decided to try to get a look through there. He glanced around the alley, found a crate that would make a good step stool. He set it down beneath the window and climbed on. He was looking into a cell, and then beyond, through the bars, he could see the open door of the cell block.

Through the doorway he saw only slivers — a piece of Bill Tilghman's desk, the marshal still seated there, and a partial view of a man standing next to him. Roper had never seen Sender. He had the killer's description and wasn't sure this was him, but it didn't really matter. Whoever he was, he was holding a gun in his hand, pointed at Tilghman — and the gun was silver.

Roper got down from the crate, walked around to the side of the building, and considered his options. He could burst through the front door and hope he could get to Sender before he shot Tilghman, but that didn't seem likely. Sender — or whoever it was — would likely pull the trigger at the first sight of Roper. He could stay outside, and wait for Sender to come out, but what if he killed Tilghman before he did that? He'd still get Sender, but he wasn't willing to trade him for the marshal.

There was only one way to go.

He went back into the alley to his crate and climbed up again. Looking through the window, he could see the hand holding the gun on Tilghman. Roper was a detective, not a sharpshooter. He used his brain more than he used his gun, but he didn't feel he had a choice.

He generally hit what he shot at, but in this case his target was a hand holding a gun, and maybe part of a forearm. Also, Tilghman was right there, presenting a big inviting target for an errant bullet. Roper was going to be allowed only one shot at this, and he had to make it count.

He drew his gun, stuck it between the bars, relaxed himself, inhaled one long, deep breath, and took the shot.

The silver gun went flying from Sender's hand, and Tilghman moved quickly, taking Sender to the floor before he could recover.

Roper withdrew his pistol, got down from the crate, and walked around to the front of the office.

Tilghman came out of the cell block, having just locked the wounded John Sender in a cell.

"What took you so damn long?" Tilghman asked. "I was tryin' to send you signals the whole time."

"I noticed a funny look on your face, and you seemed real uncomfortable, but I just thought you had the trots or something."

"Very funny. What finally tipped you off?"

"There were a few things," Roper said. "You'd never wear an empty holster. You either keep your gun on or take the whole rig off. I figured somebody had taken your gun. Also, you were calling me Roper, when you usually call me by my first name. And finally, you hate Pat Sughrue and would never call him a 'good man.'"

"He must have known you were right on his tail and figured taking a lawman hostage might buy him his life. But then why didn't he pick the sheriff?" Tilghman wondered. "If he'd shot Pat, it would have been no loss."

Roper knew Sughrue was a good lawman. He and Tilghman just didn't like each other.

"Maybe he recognized your name but not Sughrue's," Roper suggested.

"That was a nice shot, by the way," Tilghman said, "but why did you decide to just shoot the gun out of his hand? If you'd missed, he mighta killed me."

"I didn't have a choice," Roper said. "That

17

was all I could see from the window."

"Jesus," Tilghman said, "if I knew my life depended on you makin' a shot like that, I mighta been nervous. I guess I'm just lucky you're a good detective and a fair shot."

1

Denver, Colorado, months later . . .

Talbot Roper's office was on West Colfax Street that year.

Roper entered his office, mindful of the fact that the door had not been locked. Only one other person had a key to the office, and the door did not bear any of the earmarks of a door being forced. He entered with his cut-down Colt still in his shoulder holster.

He had two rooms: a reception area, and his office. The outer area had a desk and chair, file cabinets, and several extra chairs for clients to wait — if he happened to have that many. And often, he had a girl sitting at the desk.

This time, a girl he'd never seen before was seated at his reception desk. She had brown hair pinned up on top of her head and a pretty face only lightly touched with makeup. She appeared to be in her early twenties but was wearing a very businesslike suit that you would usually see on an older woman. Someone had tried to dress her for business, but she had the face and body of a girl who was made for some . . . well, friskier activity.

"Good morning," he said.

"Oh!" He'd startled her. "Can I — are you . . . Mr. Roper?" She stared at him through a pair of wire-rimmed glasses with wide, liquid eyes.

"I am," he said. "Who are you?"

"I'm Lola," she said. "Mrs. Batchelder sent me over this morning?" He hoped most of her sentences were not going to end with question marks. He hated that.

Mrs. Batchelder was the other person who had a key to his office. She had a business down the street where she trained young girls to give the businessmen in Denver what they wanted — capable office workers. Roper usually allowed her to have a key for just this reason, so her girls could let themselves in and get to work. He thought Mrs. Batchelder probably started her day earlier than anyone in Denver.

"Are you one of her star students?" he asked.

Lola frowned prettily and said, "I don't — well, I don't know . . . I think so." Pinpricks of color appeared in her cheeks, as if the question had embarrassed her. Mrs. Batchelder didn't like her girls looking like saloon girls, so she kept their makeup to a minimum.

"Has she explained your duties?"

"Oh yes," Lola said. "I know exactly what to do."

Roper didn't smell coffee, so obviously the girl didn't know *everything* she had to do.

"Can you make coffee?"

She looked crestfallen. "I'm not very good at cooking."

"Coffee isn't cooking," he said.

She looked even sadder.

"All right, never mind," he said. "Never mind. Let's just hope you're better at office work."

"I can file," she said brightly.

"That's good, but I don't have any filing for you right now."

"Well . . ."

"Just handle any clients that come in the front door," he said.

"Handle them?"

"Yes," Roper said. "Find out what they want, then come in and tell me. I'll let you know whether to bring them in or not. Got it?"

"Oh, yes, sir!"

"Good."

Roper went into his office, closing the door behind him. This room was almost three times the size of the reception area. Roper liked to be comfortable, and space was part of that. One part of the room was set up as a sitting area, with a sofa and two armchairs surrounding a cherry wood coffee table. There were paintings on the cherry wood paneled walls, which he had bought because he liked them, not because they had any particular value.

He had a large cherry wood desk, with a large, ornate green-and-gold lamp, a wide green blotter, and an expensive gold pen and letter opener set. Behind it was a large, deep leather armchair, and on either side, metal file cabinets. Behind the desk was a large window that looked out onto the street.

He liked Lola well enough. He did have some paperwork to do, which would lead to filing, but in his experience, Mrs. Batchelder's girls were not expert at filing things, especially not in alphabetical order. The reason he allowed her to keep sending him girls was that they worked for free for the experience — when they did get some work done.

He seated himself behind his big cherry wood desk and proceeded to fill out his reports on his last two cases.

After about an hour there was a tentative knock at his door.

"Come in."

Lola opened the door and stuck her head in.

"Mr. Roper, there's a man here to see you."

"Who is it?"

"He says he's a lawyer named Harwick."

Roper knew a lot of Denver lawyers, but he'd never heard of one named Harwick.

"He says he has a job for you . . . and a check."

"A check? Well, send him in, then."

"Yes, sir."

She opened the door and allowed a man in a gray suit to enter.

"Mr. Harwick?" Roper said, standing.

"Yes," the man said. "Edward Harwick. Are you Mr. Roper?"

"I am."

The two men shook hands. Harwick was as tall as Roper's six-one, but about forty pounds heavier, most of it in the gut. He wore a blue three-piece suit, a gold chain hanging from what Roper assumed would be a gold pocket watch in the vest pocket. He had a matching bowler hat, which he was holding in his hands. There were gold rings on each finger, with stones that reflected the light from the windows. Mentally, Roper's fee went up even higher than usual.

"Have a seat, please," Roper said. "I understand you have a check for me? I don't recall ever having done business with you before."

"We haven't," Harwick said. "I'm not from Denver, sir. I practice in West Virginia."

"Well, then, what brings you all this way?"

"I've come all this way to see you, sir, on behalf of my client. Howard Westover."

"Westover," Roper said, frowning. "I'm afraid I don't know that name either."

"You wouldn't," Harwick said. "Sir, I'm here to hand you a check and ask you to come back to West Virginia with me."

"For what reason?"

"To meet with my client."

"And the check?"

"It is yours, whether you come or not." To illustrate, Harwick took a brown envelope from his pocket and set it on Roper's desk. Roper left it there for the moment.

"What does your client want with me?" he asked.

"He will tell you that in West Virginia."

Roper picked up the envelope but did not look inside.

"Why me? I'm sure there are private detectives in West Virginia — or at least, closer than Denver."

"I've done research on you, sir," Harwick said. "You worked with Allan Pinkerton, both during and after the war, struck out on your own some years ago. As of today, you are generally considered to be the best private detective in the country."

"Well, that's nice to hear, but —"

"If you come back with me, there will be considerably more money than what's in that envelope."

"Well," Roper said, "I'm not usually that impressed by money, Mr. Harwick."

He opened the envelope, slid the check out, and looked at the amount written on it. Then he slid it back in.

"When do we leave?" he asked.

2

Harwick had secured them sleeping compartments on the train. The trip to West Virginia, with water stops, would take over twenty-five hours.

As the train pulled out of the station, Roper stopped by Harwick's compartment to see if he wanted to get a drink together. The lawyer looked surprised when he opened the door to Roper's knock.

"Why?"

"We still have things to talk about."

"Like what?" Harwick seemed genuinely surprised that Roper would want to have a drink with him.

"Come and have a drink, and I'll tell you."

Harwick shrugged and said, "Very well."

They went to the dining car together, got a table with ease since the kitchen was not yet serving a meal. When a white-coated waiter came over, Roper ordered a beer, and Harwick asked for a brandy.

"What is it you think we have to talk about?" Harwick asked. His eyes were on another table, where three men were playing poker.

"Well, your boss, for one," Roper said. "What's he like?"

"He's ill."

"How ill?"

Harwick blinked, tore his eyes away from the poker game, and looked at Roper with a slightly startled expression.

"I've already said more than I was supposed to," he said. "My client will fill you in on everything when we arrive."

"All right," Roper said with a sigh. His attempt to squeeze more information out of the lawyer had yielded little. Perhaps the man was actually good at his job. "Tell me about yourself, then."

"What would you like to know?"

Both men paused while the waiter set down their drinks before continuing.

"How long have you worked for Mr. Westover?"

"Almost twelve years."

"Are you from West Virginia?"

"Yes, but I practice there and in Washington, D.C."

"I'll bet that comes in handy — for your client's business, I mean."

27

Harwick sipped his brandy and did not reply. Instead, he looked over at the poker players again. Roper turned to take a look as well, then looked back at the lawyer.

"Don't even think about it," he said.

"What?" Harwick looked startled again.

"Don't think about getting into that game."

"Why not?" Harwick asked. "It would just be a way to pass the time."

"Not for them," Roper said. "The reason there are three of them is that they're waiting for a fourth, like you, to sit down so they can skin him — you."

"Skin?"

"Take," Roper said, "cheat."

"What makes you think they cheat?"

"I've ridden a lot of trains, Mr. Harwick," Roper said. "I've seen a lot of traveling poker games like that one. Maybe they won't out-and-out cheat you, but they'll work together against you. You wouldn't have a chance."

"I happen to be a very good poker player," Harwick said stiffly.

Roper could see he wasn't going to get anything out of Harwick, and he probably wasn't going to be able to talk any sense into him either. He pushed his barely touched beer away and got up.

"Thanks for having a drink with me, Harwick. If you'd like to have a meal together later, stop by my compartment."

"Fine," Harwick said, his attention already back on the poker game.

Roper left the car.

Harwick did not stop by, and when Roper got hungry, he went to the dining car and saw that the lawyer had, indeed, joined the poker game. He barely acknowledged Roper when he went by. There were others there now, dining, some together, some alone.

Roper found himself a table and ordered a steak. He sat facing the poker players so he could watch the game. It became evident while he ate his meal that the three men had found themselves a pigeon in Edward Harwick.

The three men were laughing and jostling each other, drinking — or pretending to drink — while Harwick himself was very serious about the cards in his hand. To anyone watching, it would seem he was the only one taking the game seriously, but Roper could clearly see he was being whip-sawed. The lawyer should have heeded his advice. He did not, and now he was going to pay.

Roper finished his meal and returned to his compartment.

3

Roper was reading Mark Twain's *The Prince and the Pauper*, resting on his berth, when there was a knock on his door. As he slid the door open, one hand behind him holding his gun, he was surprised to see the waiter who had served him his dinner.

"Yes?"

"Your friend, sir," the black waiter said.

"My friend?"

"The man you had a drink with? The one playing poker?"

"Oh, him. What about him?"

"I believe him to be in danger."

"In danger of losing his money, and it serves him right," Roper said. "I told him not to play with them."

"No, sir," the waiter said. "That's not it."

"What is it, then?" Roper asked.

"Well, sir . . . he's winning."

"What?"

"Yes, sir," the waiter said. "And the other

31

men are not happy."

"I guess not," Roper said. "The three of them are working together. For him to be winning, they'd have to think that he was —"

"Cheating, yes, sir."

Roper stepped back, put his gun down, donned his shoulder holster, replaced the gun in it, then put his jacket on over it.

"Let's go," he said, stepping into the hallway.

As Roper entered the dining car, he knew they were right on the verge of trouble. Other diners in the car had taken up positions around the game and were watching intently. He had to push his way through the crowd in order to get a clear view himself. Harwick was sitting with a lot of paper bills in front of him, more money than the other three men had, combined. He watched a couple of hands — which the lawyer won — and could not detect any cheating on the man's part.

"Jesus Christ!" one of the other three said, slapping his useless cards down on the table. "How is he doin' it?"

"I told you," Harwick replied. "I'm a very good poker player. I did warn you."

"Yeah," one of the other men said, "but

you didn't warn us that you would cheat."

Harwick paused in his collecting of the money and stared at the men.

"I assure you, gents, I am not cheating."

The third man leaned forward. His jacket gaped and Roper saw the gun inside. "It's the only way you can be beating us."

"You all assumed that by working together you could beat me," Harwick said. "In reality, all you could control was the way the hands were bet. None of you was good enough to deal seconds. I simply played the cards I was dealt."

The tension grew and the crowd drew back, giving the four players space to settle their argument. Some of them even rushed from the car, not wanting to be around when lead began to fly.

Roper, on the other hand, stepped forward.

"He's right."

The three men looked at Roper.

"He's better than you are," Roper said. "There's no shame in losing to a better player."

"You better mind your own business, friend," one of them said.

"This is my business, friend," Roper said. "This man and I are traveling together on business. If you kill him, I don't get paid. I can't allow that."

"You can't allow?"

"That's right."

"What do you intend to do about it?"

"That depends," Roper said, "on what you three intend to do."

"We aim to make this cheater give us back our money," one said.

"And then we're gonna teach him a lesson," a second said.

The remaining onlookers hurriedly left the car. Some remained just outside the doors at either end to peer in the windows.

"Not a chance," Roper said.

Roper knew Harwick was not armed, and yet he didn't seem overly concerned about his safety.

"Collect your winnings, Harwick," Roper said. "We're leaving."

The three men tensed, and Roper spoke quickly.

"I'll kill the first man who pulls a gun."

"There's three of us," one said.

"I know," Roper said, "and soon there'll be two . . . then one . . . and finally . . ." He shrugged.

Harwick gathered his money into his hands in a wrinkled bundle and stood up slowly. The three men watched, all straining, itching to make a move. But Roper was an unknown to them.

"Out, Harwick," Roper said.

"And you?"

"I'll be right behind you."

"Gentlemen," Harwick said, "thank you for a very interesting, and lucrative, game."

"Harwick," Roper said between clenched teeth, "go!"

The lawyer left the car.

"And now, gents, you can go back to your game."

"This ain't over," one of them said.

"What's your name, friend?" another asked.

"Roper," the detective said. He backed toward the door that Harwick had gone through. "For all our sakes, I hope this is over, but . . . until we meet again."

He turned and went out the door.

"We can't let them get away with this," Eugene Cummings said.

"Don't worry," Arthur Carl said, "we won't."

"I wanna kill that Roper, whoever he is," the third man, Ben Landau, said, "but before we kill the lawyer, I wanna know how he did it. How he cheated us."

"He didn't cheat us, you idiot," Carl said.

"He beat us fair and square with better cards."

"But . . . we still can't let him get away with it," Cummings said.

"We won't. The lawyer said he was going all the way to West Virginia. We have plenty of time."

"To do what?" Landau asked.

"To get our money back."

"But Roper . . . he must be some kind of gunman. We can't hope to beat a gunhand."

"Not face-to-face anyway," Carl said.

"You mean —"

"I mean there are other ways to kill a man like that," Carl said.

"How?" Landau asked.

"Yes, how?" Cummings echoed.

"Just give me a little time," Carl said, "and I'll come up with an answer."

4

Roper found Harwick in his compartment.

"What the hell did you think you were doing?" he demanded.

"Proving a point," Harwick said. He had dumped his money on his bed and was smoothing the bills out.

"Well, fine, you've proven it," Roper said. "You're a better poker player than they are, even working together. And now they want to kill us both."

"But . . . you made them back down."

"So they probably want to kill me even more than they want to kill you," Roper said. "You took their money, but I took their pride."

"I — I'm sorry," Harwick said. "I didn't think —"

"I know you didn't," Roper said. "I advised you not to play with them."

"Yes, you did," Harwick said. "I should have listened to you." He looked down at the money, dropped the bills he had in his hand. "What do we do now?"

"Now," Roper said, "we try to live through the remainder of this trip."

They agreed that Harwick would not leave his compartment unless Roper came to get him. They spent a quiet night, and then Roper knocked on Harwick's door.

"Breakfast?" he asked.

"I thought we were going to stay in our compartments."

"No," Roper said, "we're not going to hide. Besides, we've got to eat."

"Well, if you're sure."

"I'm more than sure," Roper said. "I'm hungry."

Harwick pulled the door to his compartment closed and followed Roper to the dining car.

As they entered, Roper saw that the three poker players were not there.

"Perhaps you scared them away," Harwick said as they sat.

"I doubt it," Roper said. "More than likely they're off making plans."

"To kill us?"

Roper nodded, waved at the waiter, the same black man who had come to his door.

"Yes, sir?"

"Flapjacks for me," Roper said. "Coffee."

"Ham and eggs," Harwick said, "and also coffee. Thank you."

"You have even more to thank him for," Roper said. "He's the one who came and got me when he saw you were in trouble."

Harwick didn't respond. He didn't seem to like having been aided by a black man — although he didn't mind having a black man wait on him.

The car was busy, but the table the three poker players had occupied was still open.

When the waiter came with their breakfast, Roper asked, "What's your name, sir?"

"Oh, you ain't gotta call me suh, suh," the man said. "My name is Roscoe."

"Well, Roscoe, is that table reserved for those three gents?"

"Yes, suh," Roscoe said. "They done reserved it as soon as they got on board."

"Which was when?" Roper asked.

"Just before you did, suh."

"Do they have compartments in the same car as we do?" Roper asked.

"They do not have compartments, suh," Roscoe said. "They are seated together in the next forward car."

"I see."

"If they're not playin' cards, suh, they're up to no good," Roscoe said.

39

"Thanks for the warning, Roscoe," Roper said.

"I'll bring more coffee, suh."

"Thank you, Roscoe."

"What do you think they'll do?" Harwick asked.

"Whatever it is, they'll do it soon," Roper said.

"So what do we do?"

"Finish our breakfast," Roper said. "By the time we're done, I'll have an idea."

"Will you?"

"Yes," Roper said, "I will."

As promised, when they had finished eating, Roper told Harwick what they were going to do.

"That puts you at risk," the lawyer said.

"And keeps you safe," Roper said.

"And that's okay with you?" Harwick asked.

"I have the feeling that keeping you alive ensures that I'll get paid," Roper said.

"But there's no guarantee you'll even take the job," Harwick said.

"Well," Roper said, "we'll both have to arrive in one piece to see what happens."

5

Cummings came back and sat across from Landau and Carl.

"Well?" Carl said. "Did you get the compartment numbers?"

"I got them."

"When do we move?" Landau asked.

"Soon," Carl said. "Very soon. We have to get this done before we arrive in West Virginia."

"And soon means . . ." Cummings asked.

Carl grinned and said, "Now."

"And how do we do it?" Landau asked.

"The lawyer first."

"Why him first?" Cummings asked.

"Because he'll be easy," Carl answered. He drew his gun. "Then we take Roper."

The other two men touched the guns in their shoulder rigs and nodded.

Roper was reading when the knock came at the door. He set the book aside.

"Yes?"

"It's the conductor, sir," a man's voice said.

Roper had spoken to the conductor on several occasions. He recognized the voice.

"Yes, what is it?"

There was a moment's hesitation and then he said, "There is a problem. I need to . . . to see you."

"All right."

Roper drew his gun, stepped back, and said, "Come on in."

The door slid open. Just for a moment the conductor stood in the doorway, and then he was pushed or yanked aside.

The three gamblers hadn't planned this assault very well. They all tried to come through the door at the same time, but only two were able to squeeze through. Of course, they were only expecting a lawyer, so they were shocked to see Roper standing there.

Roper felt he had no choice. These men all had guns in their hands. In a moment they'd recover from their surprise and start shooting.

So Roper shot first.

He shot Cummings in the belly and then, as Landau began to lift his gun, shot him in the chest.

In the hall, Arthur Carl panicked, turned, and started running. At that moment the door to Roper's compartment opened and Harwick stepped out.

"What's going —"

He stopped short when Carl ran into him. "You!"

Roper stepped out, saw Carl and Harwick tangled in the hall.

"Hold it!" he shouted.

Carl grabbed Harwick around the neck from behind and used him as a shield. Behind him the conductor cowered, afraid he'd be hit by flying lead.

"Let him go," Roper said.

Carl was in a panic, his eyes darting about in his head wildly.

"I — I only wanted my money back!" he shouted.

"And you were ready to kill for it?" Roper said. "I think it's time to drop your gun. Or we can stand just like this until we arrive at our next stop, when the law will be sent for."

"I'll kill him!" Carl pressed the barrel of his gun against Harwick's temple.

Roper had only one chance. He'd learned from a very famous doctor that you could shoot a man in a place that would instantly kill him. He wouldn't even have a chance to twitch a finger enough to pull a trigger.

"I'll give you one more chance," Roper said. "Drop it. You've got no place to go."

Carl was beyond logical thought. He'd seen his two friends shot down and was in danger himself. His panicked eyes were growing wider still, and Roper felt he had no time to wait.

He pulled the trigger. The bullet entered just beneath Carl's chin and severed his spinal cord. His body went limp and he slumped to the floor, the gun falling away from Harwick's head.

"Jesus!" Harwick said. He jumped away and looked down at Carl's body. Then he looked at Roper. "He could have shot me!"

"He could have," Roper agreed. "But now he's dead."

Roper stepped back into Harwick's compartment to check on Cummings and Landau. They were dead. He came out and checked Carl's body. He was also dead. He ejected the spent shells from his gun, replaced them with live ammunition, and then holstered it.

"Aren't you glad we exchanged compartments?" he asked.

6

Upon arrival at the first stop in West Virginia, they had to wait for the local police to board the train and ask questions about the three dead men. Roper had the conductor's testimony that they took him at gunpoint and made him knock on the door. He was also a witness that Roper had acted in self-defense. Harwick — being a West Virginian himself — had some influence, and the train was finally allowed to continue on, with Harwick and Roper aboard.

From the railroad station in Huntington, they took a buggy ride to the town of Hurricane. (Harwick said "Hurrikin," not "Hurricane.") On a perfect late summer day, beneath a clear blue sky, the town seemed peaceful and beautiful. Once they arrived there, Roper found that he had been registered in the Rockland Hotel.

"It's the best we could do here in town,"

he said to Roper, almost apologetically.

"When do I see your client?"

"Tomorrow," Harwick said. "I will go home, and you go to your room. We can both have a good meal tonight, and a good night's sleep in a real bed. In the morning, refreshed, we will ride out to the Westover home."

"How far is it?" Roper asked as they stood in front of the desk.

"Just a short buggy ride from town."

"Then why don't you meet me in the morning for breakfast?" Roper suggested. "We can have a talk before we leave."

"Talk?"

"Yes, that's right," Roper said. "I still have some questions before we take the final step to see your client."

"Do you mean — are you implying that you still might, uh, change your mind?"

"I wasn't implying that at all," Roper said, "but it is a possibility."

"I don't understand," Harwick said, looking confused. "You've come all this way."

Roper smiled and patted the attorney on the shoulder in a placating manner.

"I'll see you at breakfast, Harwick," he said and went upstairs to his room.

He didn't see why Harwick had felt the

need to apologize for the accommodations. The room was well appointed and clean. The bed was large, the mattress deep. The curtains on the window were as fancy as any he'd seen in a Denver hotel. And there was a sink with running water. What more could a man ask for? Roper had stayed in better, fancier, more expensive hotels, and much worse, but truth be told, all he needed was a clean room and bed.

And after twenty-five hours on a train, a bath.

After his bath, he dressed in clean clothing, donning a long-sleeved shirt and Levi's. Refreshed, he decided to walk around town. He stopped at the front desk and asked the clerk for the recommendation of a good restaurant.

"Even a small café," he added. "As long as it's good."

"Sir, our restaurant here is excellent —"

"I have no doubt," Roper said, "and I'm going to try it in the morning, but right now I want to go for a walk, and along the way I'm going to want something to eat."

"Of course, sir," the man said. "There's a small café a few miles from here, if you walk that far."

"I'm very healthy," Roper said, "and I'm

47

sure I'll be able to walk a few miles. Draw me a map, please."

"Yes, sir," the clerk said. "Of course."

Armed with the clerk's map, Roper began to walk. Hurricane was a small town by most definitions, but a walk of a few miles showed him several churches, many stores, and residences. Oddly, there didn't seem to be many old buildings — until he reached the "X" marked on the map. Apparently, the café the clerk sent him to was in a part of the town called Old Town.

The buildings here were much older, some wooden, some brick-and-mortar, but most of them falling down. The café was in a brick building that looked as if it had seen some recent repairs and renovations. There were fresh, new brick patches here and there, and some of its windows had been bricked up as well.

He went inside and a middle-aged woman, gray-haired and thickset, wearing a simple cotton dress, came up to him and said, "Welcome to Saint Mary's."

"Saint Mary's?"

"Yes, that's our name," she said. "We have a mission."

"This is a mission?" he asked.

"No," she said patiently, "we have a mission to see that the less fortunate people are taken care of — fed, clothed, housed. Cared for."

"I was told this was a café."

"Oh, it is," she said. "If you'd like something to eat, you're welcome."

"But . . . I'll be paying," he said.

"Of course," she said. "Please take a table. Tell me what you would like to eat, and after you're done, you may pay us."

"How much?" he asked.

She smiled and said, "However much you think the meal was worth. We operate on donations, sir."

"I see."

"What would you like?"

"Well, I've just had a very long train trip and I'd like something . . . comforting, and warm."

"Fall in West Virginia is beautiful," she told him. "It won't get very cold, but I know what you need. If you'll leave it to me?"

"Yes, of course."

"Then I shall return shortly with your meal."

Roper looked around. The café was simple, with plain walls and fixtures, nothing fancy, and tables and chairs that looked recently handmade. There were no other customers. He wondered why the desk clerk

49

would send him here, rather than other restaurants and cafés he had passed along the way.

He sat back to wait, and the woman reappeared with a coffeepot and cup. She placed both on the table, and then filled the cup for him.

"Your food will be here soon," she assured him.

"What's your name?" he asked.

"I am Sister Katherine."

"Are you . . . a nun?"

"No," she said with a shrug. "I am only a sister in that we are all brothers and sisters."

"I see."

"Let me get your food."

She went back to the kitchen and returned shortly with a big bowl of stew. As she set it in front of him, he saw great chunks of meat, squares of boiled potatoes, pearl onions, sliced carrots, and in the center of the bowl, a mound of mashed potatoes.

"Comfort food," she assured him.

"I can see that."

He picked up a chunk of meat with a spoon and put it in his mouth. It was perhaps the tenderest, tastiest meat he'd ever eaten. The mashed potatoes were creamy and delicious. The two kinds of potatoes did not seem incongruous; rather, they complemented each other.

"It's wonderful," he said.

"Thank you."

"Did you cook it?"

"Oh, no," she said. "We have several cooks, but I am not one of them."

"Why is there no one else here?"

"I don't know if you noticed," she said, "we are off the beaten path."

"Yes, that's rather obvious."

"But people find us," she assured him.

"Can you sit with me while I eat?" he asked. "Answer some questions?"

"About what?"

"About Saint Mary's," he said, "about Hurricane . . . about someone named Howard Westover. I'm here to see him, but I don't know anything about him."

"The Medal of Honor winner?" she asked, sitting across from him. "What do you want to know?"

"Everything," he said.

7

The next morning Roper was in the hotel dining room when the lawyer, Harwick, entered. The man saw him and walked quickly across the crowded room to join him. They were dressed similarly in vested suits, Roper blue, and Harwick gray.

"I'm sorry I'm late."

"Five minutes," Roper said.

"Yes," Harwick said, "very unlike me. Again, my apologies."

"It's all right."

A waitress came over, much too bright and happy at that hour of the morning, and they ordered their breakfasts.

"I went for a walk yesterday."

"Yes?"

"Found out a few things."

Harwick frowned.

"Like what?"

"Like Howard Westover is a Medal of Honor winner from the Civil War."

"That's no secret."

"It was to me."

"No," Harwick said, "not a secret. Just something you would have found out later today."

"I see."

"Who told you?"

"A lady named Sister Katherine."

"From Saint Mary's?"

"That's right."

"How did you get to Saint Mary's?"

"It was recommended to me."

"By who?"

Roper sat back in his chair.

"I'm not sure I want to answer that right now."

The waitress came back with their eggs, setting the plates down in front of them.

"All right," Harwick said. "I am not going to ask or answer any more questions."

"Why not?"

"It's not my place."

"And whose place is it?"

"You'll find out later today."

"And what if I won't move from here until you do answer some more questions?"

"You took the check, cashed it," Harwick said, "and you came all this way. That would seem silly, don't you think?"

Roper hesitated, then said, "Yeah, probably."

"So let's eat," Harwick said, "and then we can go."

Harwick had a buggy waiting for them outside the hotel. Roper would rather have ridden a horse, but he climbed aboard and allowed Harwick to drive.

A few miles outside of town he spotted the house in the distance. A three-story antebellum mansion with four great white columns, galleries rather than balconies, large windows, and ivy-covered walls. There were even a couple of turrets, giving it a small castle-like appearance.

"Very impressive," he said.

"Built just after the war," Harwick said, "when Howard Westover came back from the field."

"Was he from here originally?"

"Yes," Harwick said. "His wife was waiting for him here, living in a much smaller house in town. They had this built and moved out here. They've lived here ever since."

"The war's been over a long time," Roper said. "Twenty years."

"Yes," Harwick said and nothing else.

He drove the buggy up to the front of the

house and stepped down. Roper followed. Harwick led him up the stairs to the front porch to the front door and opened it without knocking.

"Wait here, please," Harwick said in an entry foyer that was larger than most of the houses Roper had seen in town. "I'll find Victoria."

"Victoria?"

"Mrs. Westover."

"The wife?"

"That's right."

"I thought I was here to see Howard Westover?"

"Just . . . wait here. It will all become clear to you soon."

"All right," Roper said. "As you said, I've come this far."

"Thank you."

Harwick walked into the bowels of the house and disappeared. Roper looked around. To the left was a large dining room, with an expensive cabinet filled with bone china, and a long, wooden oak table with a fine sheen to it. To the right, there was an opulently furnished parlor, with stuffed armchairs and a large sofa, with curtains of red-and-gold brocade on all the windows. Above him was a great crystal-and-gold chandelier.

There was a stairway leading to the second floor. Roper didn't know how he'd done it, but somehow Harwick had gotten up there. He came down the steps now, leading a woman.

She appeared to be in her late forties, a handsome woman, tall, slender, with black hair that had a gray steak through it. She was wearing a floor-length dress that looked simple but was, Roper was sure, expensive.

When they reached the bottom, they approached Roper.

"Mr. Roper, this is Mrs. Howard Westover — Victoria Westover."

"Mr. Roper," she said, extending her hand. "Thank you so much for coming to see me."

He shook her hand. "I thought I was coming to see your husband."

"Later," she said. "But you have actually come here to see me."

"So the check was from you?"

"Yes. And I will pay you the same amount again."

"To do what?"

"Well, to start with, to listen. Do you drink tea?" she asked.

"I've been known to."

"Then let's have tea and talk. Edward, will you join us?"

"Of course, Victoria."

From the look on Harwick's face, it was clear to Roper that the attorney was in love with his employer. It was also clear that she did not reciprocate. To her, he was just that — an employee.

"This way," she said.

8

Victoria Westover walked them through the dining room into a glass-enclosed back porch. It looked out onto a back area full of lush green grass and shade-giving trees, and farther out beyond that, a gazebo. They were seated in expensive wicker furniture, and a woman came in and served tea and cakes, setting them down on a glass-top table.

"Thank you, Miriam."

The older woman nodded and left.

"Mr. Roper, my husband won the Medal of Honor in the Civil War."

"That much I do know."

She looked at Harwick quickly.

"I didn't tell him," the lawyer said. "He went to Saint Mary's."

"Oh."

"Is that a bad thing?" Roper asked.

"Saint Mary's is . . ." Victoria began, then trailed off. "Well, that's neither here nor there."

"With all due respect, Mrs. Westover," Roper asked, "what is here or there?"

"Mr. Roper," she said, sitting forward and clasping her hands, "the government might be taking my husband's medal back."

"Why would they do that?"

"I don't know," she said. "That is what I want you to find out. I want you to go to Washington, find out what the Army is doing, and discover what needs to be done to make sure . . . to guarantee my husband dies a Medal of Honor winner."

"Dies?"

Victoria looked at Harwick, who nodded.

"Come with me, Mr. Roper," she said. The lawyer started to rise, but she said, "Edward, stay and drink your tea. Someone should. After all, Miriam made it."

He nodded and sat down.

"Mr. Roper?"

He followed her from the room.

Victoria Westover took Roper back to the foyer and up the stairs.

"Are we going to see your husband?"

"Yes."

"Why didn't he come down to have tea?"

"You'll see."

Upstairs he followed her down a hallway to a door, where she stopped and turned to face him.

"He's inside," she said. "Please don't react when you see him."

"React? How?"

"Just . . . don't act shocked. He . . . he doesn't like it."

"All right."

She nodded, then opened the door.

"Mr. Roper, this is my husband, Howard Westover."

Roper entered and saw a man seated in a wheelchair. A sturdy-looking woman in her forties was feeding him something that looked like oatmeal.

Roper guessed that if he had known Howard Westover before, he might have been shocked at the man's appearance. The clothes he was wearing seemed to hang on his frame, which looked like loose skin on large bones. His cheekbones were sharp, his eyes sunken. He looked eighty, not fifty. Eyeing the man's frame, Roper assumed at one time Westover must have been well over six feet tall and was probably strapping. There was little of that man left, and now the Army wanted to take away his medal.

"Mr. Roper," Westover said. His voice was a rasp, and it seemed painful for him to speak.

"Polly, continue to feed him," Victoria

said. "I'll talk with him later."

She turned. "Mr. Roper?"

Roper turned to follow her, thought he should say goodbye to her husband, but finally just wordlessly slipped from the room.

Out in the hall she stopped, hugging herself as if she was cold.

"He came home injured," she said. "Since that time his health has simply deteriorated. Worse and worse every year." She looked at him. "He's just wasting away. The only thing he has left is that medal. To tell you the truth, I don't care if they take it away from him after he dies, just not before."

"Why tell him any of this?"

"Because they'll make a ceremony out of it," she said. "That's the way the Army — the government — operates. He'll know." She put her hand on his arm and squeezed tightly. "I can't have that, Mr. Roper. I can't. I need your help."

"Mrs. Westover," he said, "let's go back downstairs and talk."

9

They went downstairs, found Harwick pouring himself another cup of tea and eating a second cake. Roper and Victoria sat back down.

"Mrs. Westover —" Roper began.

"Victoria," she said. "Please."

"All right, Victoria . . . why me? I'm a detective. Why wouldn't you send your lawyer to Washington for this?"

"Because I don't have the best lawyer in the country working for me, Mr. Roper," she said. Roper looked at Harwick, who didn't seem to react. "But if you do this for me, I will have the best detective in the country. I need the best. I need a man who will do what must be done to make sure my husband remains a Medal of Honor winner."

Roper looked at Harwick, who seemed more concerned with his tea cakes than with the fact that his reputation was being impugned.

"Will you do it?" she asked.

"Victoria . . . let me think about it overnight," Roper said. "I'll give you my answer
in the morning. Is that all right?"

"That's fine, Mr. Roper. Thank you."

Harwick drove Roper back to his hotel in
silence, but when they arrived and stepped
down, he said to Roper, "May I buy you a
drink? I'd like to talk to you about something."

"Sure. You want to come inside?"

They went into the bar that was attached
to the hotel. It was small, with half a dozen
tables and a bar that was barely six feet
long. Based on its size and appearance, it
was meant to serve guests rather than the
public. It was still early, so there were plenty
of places at the bar and tables to be had.
They got a beer each and took them to a
table.

"What's on your mind, Harwick?"

"I would like to try to influence your decision about whether or not to go to Washington, D.C."

"You want to try to talk me into it?" Roper
asked. "I'm going to give it some thought
tonight —"

"No, sir, you don't understand," Harwick

63

said. "I'd like you not to go."

Roper took a sip of beer while studying the attorney.

"Why would you want me not to go, Harwick? Victoria is your client."

"Yes, she is," Harwick said. "She's also my . . . my friend. I don't want her to be hurt."

"It seems to me all she's been going through for years is hurt," Roper said. "It also seems to me when her husband dies, the hurt will stop — that is, unless they take away his Medal of Honor. Then the hurt will go on and on for her."

"No, you don't understand," Harwick said. "The government won't relent on this. No matter how hard she tries."

"You think she'll be hurt more by the effort?" Roper asked.

"I do, yes."

"Harwick, what do you know that you're not telling me?"

The man looked around nervously, then back at Roper. He played with his beer mug but never took a drink, yet he was licking his lips as if they were dry.

"During the war," he said, "there was a group of two hundred men who were all awarded the Medal of Honor at the same time. Do you know what they did?"

"No," Roper said, "what did they do to deserve the honor?"

"They reenlisted."

"That's it?"

"That's all. The Army is going to take their medals back."

"Seems to me they should," Roper said. "What did Westover get his medal for?"

"I don't know."

"And you're afraid Victoria will find that her husband got the medal for something as mundane as simply reenlisting?"

"Perhaps," Harwick said. "I'm not sure — I don't know — she might already know why he got it. Mr. Roper, I just don't think it's a good idea for you to go to D.C."

"Well, Mr. Harwick, I did promise Mrs. Westover I would think about it overnight, and I will. I'll give her my answer in the morning."

"Well . . . all I ask is that you please also give what I said some thought."

"Sure," Roper said. "I'll think about it."

"Yes, all right," Harwick said. He stood up. "I must be going."

"I'll stay awhile," Roper said, "finish my beer."

"Yes, of course. We'll, uh, talk tomorrow morning, then."

"Yes," Roper said. "Tomorrow morning."

Harwick stood to leave but hesitated.

"Something else?" Roper asked.

"I . . . never thanked you properly for saving my life on the train."

"That's okay, Harwick," Roper said. "It was my job."

"Still . . . thank you."

As the attorney left the bar, Roper couldn't help feeling that there was something else at play here. Something he wasn't aware of.

10

That night Talbot Roper did a lot of hard thinking in his room.

Part of Roper's reluctance to take the job was that he'd have to go to D.C. It had been a lot of years since he'd been to Washington. Also a lot of years since he'd had dealings with the government.

But then there was the money. He'd lied in Denver when he told Harwick money didn't impress him. Numbers with lots of zeroes impressed him quite a bit, and Victoria Westover was waving a lot of zeroes in his face.

And then there was his own curiosity. What had Howard Westover won his medal for? If he deserved it, he should be able to keep it; he should be able to die a Medal of Honor winner.

The image of Westover in the wheelchair being fed oatmeal came back to him. He shook his head to dispel it, walked to the window to look out at the dark street below.

He turned, looked back at the few feet he'd walked to get there from the bed. It was something Howard Westover couldn't do anymore.

Roper decided to go to D.C., at least to see what the government was planning to do and why. Decision made, he returned to the bed and picked up the Mark Twain novel he'd been carrying with him on his journey. He'd read for a little while to calm his mind of the day's events before turning in for the night.

In the morning Roper had breakfast in the dining room. He was not disappointed when the lawyer, Harwick, did not appear. There was something about the man he didn't like, and it had to do with the way he looked at his employer, Victoria Westover.

"Anything else, sir?" the waiter asked.

Roper looked at the man. He was middle-aged and performed his job as if he had been doing it forever.

"What's your name, waiter?"

"Andrew, sir."

"Are you from Hurricane?" Roper asked him.

"Yes, sir, been here all my life. It's a lovely place to live."

"I met two of your citizens yesterday, Howard and Victoria Westover."

"Yes, sir, they do live inside our town limits. Nice people."

"Are they?"

"Yes, sir."

"Too bad about what's happened to him, though, isn't it?"

"Indeed, sir. He was a hero in the war, and he has had to pay for it the rest of his life, just . . . deteriorating."

"Mrs. Westover is quite a woman," Roper said. "Some wives would have left rather than face years of caring for an invalid."

"He has not always been an invalid, sir," the waiter said, "but you are quite correct. She's a strong woman. We in Hurricane are quite proud to have them living here."

"Thank you, Andrew."

"Yes, sir."

As the waiter withdrew, Roper wondered if his opinion was held by others in Hurricane. He decided to take another walk around town, performing his own survey as he went.

He paid his bill and took to the streets.

Roper stopped in the shops — hardware, gunsmith, tanners, mercantile — and talked to the shopkeepers about their town. They

69

all seemed to love it, as well as their neighbors. He stopped in a couple of saloons, but even men in their cups had nothing but good things to say about Hurricane, and about the Westovers.

He stopped in a café for coffee and a slice of pie and listened to the others talk about their families, their businesses, their lives. Hurricane seemed to be populated by people who were happy with their lot in life. In other words, a very strange place, indeed.

When he returned a couple of hours later, he found Harwick sitting on the front porch, waiting for him.

"You missed breakfast," Roper pointed out.

"Yes, I'm sorry about that," Harwick said. "I had some work to finish and thought I would give you some more time to think."

"Well, I appreciate that," Roper said. "I actually put that time to good use, took another walk around your fair town."

"Have you come to a decision?"

There was another chair on the porch so Roper pulled it over and sat.

"The folks in this town think very highly of Howard Westover."

"Yes, they do."

"They like having a Medal of Honor winner as one of their citizens."

70

"I suppose they do."

"And they quite admire Victoria."

"As they should," the lawyer said. "She's a fine woman."

"Harwick, is there something else going on here?" Roper asked.

"I don't know what you mean."

"I'm just wondering if there's anything else I should be aware of."

"I believe you are in full possession of all the facts you need to make your decision."

"You're probably right."

Harwick waited a beat, then said, "And?"

"You can tell your employer that I'll go to D.C., see what I can find out."

"And beyond that?"

"Beyond that, we'll see. It depends on what I find out while I'm there."

"You'll need to know who to see while you're there," Harwick said.

"That's all right," Roper said. "I have my own connections in D.C."

"When will you leave?"

"I'll catch the next train," Roper said.

"Would you like me to purchase that ticket for you?" Harwick asked.

"No, I can take care of that myself. It's not a long or expensive trip."

"I'll tell Mrs. Westover your decision," the lawyer said.

"And tell her I'll come back here with whatever I find out," Roper said.

"I'll inform her."

"And if you don't mind, I'll keep my room here."

"That is no problem," Harwick said.

"I'll let you know when I get back," Roper said. "We'll talk again, Harwick."

"Yes, sir," Harwick said. "I'll look forward to it."

Roper thought that was a lie, and probably not the first one he'd been told by the lawyer.

11

The train ride to D.C. was much shorter than the ride from Denver. In fact, Roper could have rented a horse and ridden to D.C., but he wanted to get there more quickly. His curiosity was getting the better of him.

When he reached Washington, he went to the Georgetown Hotel and got himself a room at his own expense. The Georgetown was one of the finest hotels in D.C. He got himself a simple room with the usual furniture, but it was all well made with good wood, though not the best. Had he gotten a suite, he would have been ensconced in opulence. He knew opulence, but was not always comfortable with it. And since he was paying for his own room, a simple one would do.

He had dinner in the hotel dining room, a thick steak with all the trimmings. The tables were covered with good white tablecloths, and the silverware was old, but kept clean. The room served the locals as well as the guests. Some of them were regulars there. He could tell by the way they looked at him, wondering who he was. In turn, he did not wonder who they were. He was satisfied that he could see them. He sat so he could see everyone in the room, knew where they all were. And he could tell who was armed, and who was not.

After dinner he went to the front desk and said he wanted to send a telegram.

"Our telegraph key opens at eight in the morning, sir," the clerk said.

"That's fine," Roper said. "I can write it out now, and you can send it first thing."

"Yes, sir, we can do that."

The clerk supplied Roper with a pencil and paper, and the detective wrote out a brief telegram.

The clerk read it and said, "Sir, you're sending this telegram right —"

"Yes," Roper said, cutting him off, "right here in town. I should get a quicker response that way, don't you think?"

"Well . . . yes, sir."

"Fine," Roper said. "Send it. If a reply comes in before I come down to breakfast, have it brought to my room."

"Yes, sir."

Roper went to his room, read some more Twain, and went to bed early.

He came down the next morning early for breakfast, wearing a suit, sans vest. He nodded to the clerk as he passed.

The dining room was full, but he managed to appropriate the same table as the night before. The diners eating breakfast were a different lot from those who had been having dinner. There had been more men the night before. This morning the men had women with them. Some of the tables held two or three women eating breakfast together. The women looked at him in a different way than the men had the night before. Still with interest, curiosity, but a different kind. When he caught them looking, he smiled, and they turned away, but did so with small smiles of their own.

While he was eating breakfast, a bellman came in with the reply to his telegram.

"When did it come?" he asked.

"Minutes ago, sir."

"Thank you," Roper said and tipped the man.

"Yes, sir, thank you, sir."

He unfolded the telegram and read it. He had a ten o'clock appointment at a building on Dupont Circle. He poured himself some more coffee.

He presented himself at Dupont Circle at exactly 10 a.m. He stood in front of a large stone building four stories high, with no symbols on the building to indicate what — or whom — it housed.

"Talbot Roper," he said to the soldier in the lobby.

"Yes, sir," the soldier told him. "You're expected. Please follow me."

The building appeared to have been constructed only a few years before, and was equipped with one of Mr. Otis's new steam-operated elevators. An operator took them to the third floor. Roper had been in elevators before, but still found himself holding his breath until the doors opened again.

Roper followed the soldier down a long hallway, past doors with names and titles on them, to a blank door.

"Inside, sir."

"Do I knock?" Roper asked.

"No need, sir."

"Thank you."

The soldier positioned himself to the left of the door, and Roper was sure he would still be there when he came out.

He opened the door and entered. There was nothing in the room but a desk, two chairs, and a man sitting behind the desk. The man was in his forties, with black hair that came to a widow's peak, and sparse eyebrows over intense blue eyes. He had a definite air of authority about him, even though he wore a simple blue suit with no insignia.

"Tal."

"Donny."

The man smiled. "I haven't been called that in years. Everybody around here calls me Donald, or Mr. White, or sir."

"I'll call you whatever you like."

Donald White stood up and smiled. "From an old friend, Donny is just fine."

Roper approached the desk, and the two men shook hands warmly. They had worked together during the war under Pinkerton, both learning at the feet of the great detective. They were equals then, until Roper left to start his own agency. They had seen each other only sporadically since. In the meantime, White had worked his way up the government ladder and was currently the head of what was now called the Secret Service.

"Have a seat," White said. "I can't offer you anything because you're not really here."

"I understand."

"What can I do for you?"

"Donny, I have a client who is a Medal of Honor winner."

"Uh-oh."

"What?" Roper asked.

"You heard about what the government is planning to do." It wasn't a question.

"So it's true?"

"That the government has decided to rescind a large number of medals that were given out during and after the war? Yes."

"Jesus, Donny —"

"I don't know if you heard how many of the medals were presented erroneously, capriciously —"

"I heard about two hundred that were presented to men simply for re-upping."

"Perfect example," White said.

"That's fine," Roper said. "I can understand it in that instance, but what about some of the others?"

"I can't really discuss this, Tal," White said. "In fact, I'm not even involved officially."

"I didn't think you were," Roper said, "but you were the person I thought I could get in to see the quickest."

White spread his hands and said, "Obviously you were right."

Roper studied his friend. Working in the

government behind a desk had added some pounds to the man, but he still appeared to be in good shape. And he still seemed to have a mind of his own, rather than having become a government puppet, like a lot of the men Roper had known in the past.

"All right," Roper said, "let's talk about a specific case."

"Your client."

"Howard Westover."

White frowned. "I don't know the name."

"I have to admit I don't know exactly why he received his medal," Roper said. "It wasn't a question I wanted to ask his wife, under the circumstances."

"What are the circumstances?"

Roper told Donald White about Westover's condition, how he was wounded in the war and had continued to deteriorate over the years, to the point where he was now in a wheelchair.

"That's unfortunate," White commented. "What do you want me to do, Tal?"

"For now I'd just like you to look into the circumstances of Westover's medal. Let me know how and why he was awarded it, and whether or not he's in danger of losing it."

White sat back in his chair and regarded his friend for a few moments. "I suppose I can do that. You're at the Georgetown?"

"Yes."

"Then I'll look into it and get back to you tomorrow," the man promised.

"Should I come back here?"

"No," White said, "I'll come to you."

"At my hotel?"

"Tomorrow night I'll pick you up for supper," White said. "I'll take you to my favorite restaurant. Six o'clock."

"Right out in the open?"

"Why not?" White spread his arms. "Just two old friends having dinner."

"Well, that's fine with me," Roper said, standing, "as long as the government is paying."

White smiled. "Naturally."

12

When Roper came out of White's office, the soldier was still standing there, as expected.

"Done, sir?" he asked.

"Yes."

"This way."

The soldier showed him back to the main door.

"Thank you," Roper said.

"No problem, sir."

Outside, Roper walked to the corner, where he was able to wave down a passing cab. He told the young driver to take him to the Georgetown Hotel. After five minutes he sat forward, took his cut-down Colt from his holster, and pressed it to the back of the man's neck.

"This isn't the way to the Georgetown."

"No, sir."

"Where are you taking me?"

"Somebody wants to see you, Mr. Roper."

"And who might that be?"

"Colonel Adam Sanderson."

"Sanderson," Roper said, sitting back.

"Yes, sir. He ordered me to pick you up and take you to him."

"You one of his men?"

"Yes, sir. Corporal Tom Prince."

"He tell you who I am?"

"Yes, sir, and what you look like."

"When did you get these orders?"

"About fifteen minutes ago, sir."

Roper put his gun away. The last time he had seen Sanderson, the man was a captain.

"How many birds has he got?"

"Two, sir," Prince said. "Word is the third one is on the way."

"He must be . . . what? Sixty?"

"The colonel is in excellent health, sir."

"I'm sure he is," Roper said.

"We're almost there, sir," Prince said. "Do you want me to turn back?"

"Do I have that option?"

"Oh, yes, sir. The colonel told me you'd tumble to what I was doin' right away. He said if you wanted me to turn back, I was to do so. It was up to you."

"Did he also tell you I might kill you?"

"Uh, yes, sir," Prince said.

"And still you agreed to pick me up?"

"I didn't agree, sir," Price said. "I wasn't given a choice. I was ordered."

Roper thought a moment. He hadn't been in Dupont Circle long, but someone had gotten the word to Sanderson and he'd acted quickly.

"No, that's okay, soldier. Keep going."

"Yes, sir. Thank you, sir. And thank you for not shooting me."

"You're welcome, soldier," Roper said. "You're very welcome."

The man was standing on the banks of the Potomac, staring out at the water. He was in full uniform. If his back had not been to Roper, the detective would have seen his eagle insignias shining in the sun.

"There he is, sir," Prince said, reining the horse in.

"I see him, soldier." Roper looked around, didn't see anybody else. "He's covered, isn't he?"

"No, sir," Prince said.

"You sure?"

"The colonel told me it would be just you and him," Prince said. "He even said I was to drive away and come back in twenty minutes."

"Twenty?"

"Yes, sir."

"All right." Roper stepped down from the cab.

"Sir?"

"Yes?"

"Your gun?"

Roper turned to look at Prince. The man was pointing a .45 at him.

"What are your orders, soldier?"

"To relieve you of your weapon, sir."

"And if I don't give it up?"

"You don't get to see the colonel."

"He's the one who wants to see me."

"These are not the colonel's orders, sir."

"Whose then?"

"His aide, Captain Morressy."

Roper did not know that name, but it appeared the man was only trying to safeguard his commanding officer's life.

"Yeah, okay." He handed his weapon over. Prince holstered his own .45.

"Thank you, sir."

"Sure, soldier. Thanks for not shooting me."

Prince smiled, turned, picked up the reins, and shook them at his horse. The cab started off. Roper waited until it had driven out of sight, then turned and walked toward the river's edge, and the colonel.

13

Roper walked to the colonel, who continued to stare out at the running river.

"It's beautiful," he said.

"Yes, it is."

Sanderson looked at Roper over his shoulder.

"It's a famous river, the Potomac, but then I'll bet you've seen many famous rivers. Your work takes you all over the country."

"I have. The Hudson, the Mississippi, the Missouri, the Colorado . . ."

The colonel turned to face Roper. Sixty had been a kind guess. The man looked to be in his late sixties — gray, dry-skinned, wrinkled, he also looked tired. Very tired. Roper wondered how much clout the man really had anymore.

"What brings you to Washington, Roper?" he asked.

"Why do you want to know, Colonel?"

"It's my job to safeguard this country."

Roper laughed. "From me?"

"From anyone." The colonel frowned at Roper's suit jacket. "Did he disarm you?"

"Yes."

"I told him not to."

"He had orders."

"Not from me."

"You were willing to trust me this close to you with a gun?"

"Yes."

"Why?"

"Because you know I'm more in hell alive than dead," the colonel said. "You were there, during the war. You saw me, you know that I reveled in it. I'm a fighting soldier, Roper. And when I'm not fighting, I'm in hell. I'm . . . dying here in Washington. Dying . . . you know it."

"I'm not here about that."

"Then what?"

"I'm trying to find out about the government's plan to recall certain Medals of Honor."

Sanderson frowned again.

"Why would you care about that?" he asked. "You never got one."

"This isn't about me," Roper said. "I have a client."

"That's right," Sanderson said. "You're some kind of detective now, aren't you?"

"A private detective, yes."

"Like Pinkerton."

"I'd be lucky if I was as good a detective as Allan Pinkerton was."

"An egomaniac, that man," Sanderson said with a far-away look in his eyes. "He was given too much authority during the war. It went to his head."

Roper didn't rush to Pinkerton's defense. That wasn't why he was there either.

"What were you doing at Dupont Circle?" the colonel asked. "Who were you seeing?"

"I can't say, sir."

"Confidentiality?"

"Yes, sir."

Sanderson studied Roper for a few moments, then turned and looked out at the river again. Roper moved up next to him and also took in the river. It was blue, bluer than most rivers he'd seen — the Mississippi and the Missouri were muddy brown — but they all ran the way the Potomac was running today.

"When did we last see each other, Roper?" the colonel asked.

"Allan Pinkerton's funeral."

"That's right," the soldier said. "What a farce. To die from biting your tongue."

It was an odd way for a man like Pinkerton to die, biting his own tongue in a fall and then succumbing to infection. His sons, William and Robert, took over the agency then.

"We didn't talk much then, did we?"

"Well, sir," Roper said, "we've never talked much. You never did like me."

"Yes, you're correct," Sanderson said. "And you? How did you feel about me?"

"I respected you, sir," Roper said, "and I still do."

"But you didn't like me?"

Roper hesitated, then said, "Well, you never gave me much reason to like you."

"It was never you, Roper," Sanderson said. "It was your methods. I've always thought they were . . . dubious at best."

"But effective."

"Yes, there was that."

"We were at war, sir," Roper said. "You and I have never agreed on the rules of war."

"That's correct," the colonel said. "I believe there are rules, and you do not."

Roper had nothing to say to that. There was no argument there.

"I'm getting old," Sanderson said after a few moments. "As a result, I believe I'm mellowing."

"That couldn't be," Roper said.

Sanderson smiled. "I heard you were here, at Dupont Circle, and I had a knee-jerk reaction. I brought you here — you came here willingly once you knew it was me, is that correct?"

"Yes, sir."

Sanderson looked at him. "You're still a young man with a lot of life ahead of you."

"Yes, sir."

"I envy you."

Again, Roper had no reply.

"Young Prince will be along soon to take you to your hotel," Sanderson said. He took a deep breath and lifted his chin. "I still have a lot of influence in Washington, Roper."

"I don't doubt that, sir."

"Whatever you're doing, if I can help, don't hesitate to call on me."

Stunned, Roper said, "Thank you, sir."

Roper heard the carriage behind him. The colonel seemed to have nothing more to say. He was engrossed in whatever he saw out on the river.

Roper turned and walked back to the carriage.

14

On the ride back, Roper asked, "How long has he been like that?"

He thought Prince might respond, "Like what?" but the young man was better than that.

"It's been a while, sir," he said. "The captain looks after him pretty well, makes sure he doesn't get himself in trouble."

"I see."

"The captain would like to see you before you leave," Prince said.

"Is this up to me again, Corporal?" Roper asked. "Or a command?"

"No, sir," Prince said. "The captain just said to let you know."

"Well, why not?" Roper asked. "All I'm doing is having supper with an old friend tomorrow. I'm free all day today."

"I'll tell him, sir."

"If he wants, he can send you to pick me up again, at my hotel," Roper said. "I expect to be there the whole time."

"Not interested in seeing Washington, sir?" Prince asked.

"Corporal, I've seen all of Washington I ever want to see."

"It's changed, sir."

"Not enough," Roper said. "Not nearly enough."

Roper was reading the Twain novel when there was a knock on his door. He expected to see Corporal Prince there, but the man standing in the doorway was a captain. He was over six feet tall, about forty-five years old, and wore his uniform — and the collection of medals that adorned his chest — proudly. He had slate gray eyes that stared coldly through Roper.

"Mr. Roper?"

"That's right."

"My name is Captain Morressy."

"I figured."

"I hope you don't mind that I came here," Morressy said. "I wanted our meeting to be in private."

Roper deciphered that to mean the captain did not want to be seen in public with him.

"Doesn't bother me if it doesn't bother you, Captain," Roper said. "Come on in."

The captain came in and closed the door

behind him.

"I've got nothing to offer you in the way of a drink," Roper said.

"That's all right," the Captain said. "I don't plan to be here long, Mr. Roper. We can dispense with any polite pleasantries."

"Just long enough to say your piece, huh?"

"Precisely."

There was one armchair in the room, and Roper sat in it.

"All right, then," he said. "Have at it."

"You saw Colonel Sanderson today."

"I did."

"Then you know."

"Know what? That he's mellowed? That he's lost some of his sharpness?"

"The colonel is ill, sir."

"I thought as much," Roper said. "He doesn't look good at all."

"That's physically," the captain said, "and he has become somewhat . . . frail. But I refer to his mental state."

"Yes, I saw that, too."

The captain paced while he spoke. The shine on his boots was almost painful. As he stared at Roper, his face remained expressionless, as if carved from granite.

"I am generally able to shield the colonel from contact with others," Morressy said, "but somehow, he slipped away today."

"He seemed to have had a pretty good guard dog in Corporal Prince," Roper commented.

"Yes, Prince is a good lad," Morressy agreed. "It was he who told me you were to see the colonel today."

"I figured that, too. Do you want to know what else I figure?"

"Yes, I do," the captain said. He stopped pacing and faced Roper. "Tell me what the country's greatest detective has deduced."

"I figure you're worried I'll talk about what I saw today," Roper said. "I figure you came here to warn me, or threaten, or cajole, or whatever, not to talk about the condition I saw the colonel in."

"He needs to stay in the service long enough to get his third bird," Morressy said. "That's all. It's probably only a matter of months."

"Well, Captain," Roper said. "I'm not about to ruin the man's chances. That's not what I came to Washington to do."

"But you and he . . . he's told me about you, that you weren't friends."

"We were never friends," Roper said, "and we never will be."

The captain seemed surprised, the first crack in his countenance.

"But . . . he's a great man."

"I respect him," Roper said, "but he's not a great man. Never was, never will be. On that, you and I disagree."

"How can you —"

"However," Roper said, cutting the man off, "I pledge not to say anything."

"Can I depend on that?"

"Yes, you can."

The captain stared at him.

"Depend on it, or kill me to shut me up, Captain. Your choice," Roper said. "I assume you wouldn't hesitate to kill for Colonel Sanderson."

"No, I would not," the man said. "But in this instance, I don't believe I'll have to."

"I'm glad to hear that."

"I think we are done here," the captain said, and headed for the door.

As the door closed behind him, Roper said, "Yep, I think we are."

15

Roper had a leisurely breakfast the next morning, once again in the hotel dining room. He hadn't been kidding when he told Corporal Prince he'd seen enough of Washington D.C. He was only there to find out what he needed to, and then he'd be gone, and he didn't intend to come back. Roper had never liked brass — respected some of them, but never liked them — and he detested politicians and their backroom deals.

After breakfast he took his book outside to the front of the hotel and read it sitting in a chair.

At lunchtime he went back into the dining room. After that he sent a telegram to his office, on the off chance that Lola — or someone else from Mrs. Batchelder's school — would read it. After that he went back to the porch to read.

Around 3 p.m. he'd put the book down

and was watching the people walk and ride by. The clerk came out and handed a telegram to him.

"Thanks."

He unfolded it. It was Lola, telling him it was nice to know where he was and that no one was looking for him. That was fine with him. He wasn't losing any other business while being in Washington. That would have just been adding insult to injury.

He went back to his book but was interrupted when a shadow fell across the pages. He looked up and saw Corporal Prince standing there, in uniform.

"Corporal," he said, putting the book down in his lap, "who wants to see me now?"

"No one, sir," Prince said. "I'm here for me. On my own time."

"Is that a fact? And what's on your mind?"

"Sir, I've heard stories about you, during the war, working for Mr. Pinkerton. And some of the things you've done since the war."

"I'm sure everything you've heard about me in Washington has not been good."

"No, sir," Prince said, "but I know when people are speaking Washington."

" 'Speaking Washington,' " Roper repeated. "I like that. "Do you want to get a drink, Corporal?"

"I would like to, sir, but I am due back on duty soon," Prince said. "I just wanted to stop by and say . . . well, if there's anything I can do to help —"

"With what, Corporal?"

"With . . . whatever you're working on," Prince said, "whatever brought you here. If I can help, I'd be available."

"Would you be?"

"Yes, sir, I would."

"Well, that's good to know, Corporal," Roper said. "Good to know."

"You can contact me through the captain," Prince said, then left, having had his say.

Roper had the feeling he knew a better way to contact the corporal if he needed to than through the captain.

At five o'clock, he went to his room to change for supper.

At five fifty-five, an open carriage pulled up in front. Donald White was sitting in it, and a young man was driving. Roper had no doubt the man was a soldier, but he was not in uniform. He reminded Roper of young Prince, but it was not him.

"Well," White yelled, "you gonna just sit there?"

Roper stood up from his chair and walked

to the carriage.

"You've had a busy day," White said.

"Just been sitting in that chair," Roper said.

"I mean yesterday," White said. "Come on, get in."

Roper climbed in and the carriage started forward.

"Have you been watching me?" Roper asked.

"Not exactly," White said, "but I've got eyes everywhere."

"So you know —"

"I don't know shit for sure, Tal," White said. "You can tell me all about it over a nice thick steak."

They sat quietly for the next few miles and listened to the sound of the wheels on the cobblestone streets.

White took him to a steak house called The Texas Steer. It was a large room with high ceilings, hardwood floors, and rough-hewn wooden tables and chairs.

At the door a man wearing a suit greeted them.

"Mr. White. Nice to see you back."

"Thank you, Winston. A quiet table, please?"

"Yes, sir, of course."

They followed Winston across the large expanse of the room. Along the way several men greeted White, and a few of them even stuck their hands out to shake.

"Thank you, Winston," White said to the man when they reached a table in the back from where they'd be able to see the entire room.

"Maxwell will be with you shortly, sir."

The man walked away and Roper looked across the table at White.

"Winston? Maxwell?"

"I doubt those are their real names," White said. "But they make sure I have an excellent dining experience every time I come here."

Roper looked around. There were still some diners looking at them, no doubt wondering who White was to receive such preferential treatment.

"Who do they think you are?"

"Some bullshit government bureaucrat," White said. "They don't know what I do, just that I do it for the government. For that reason, they want to think they're my friends."

The waiter came over and White ordered two steak dinners and beer. The beer came first, in thick glass mugs with stems.

"To your health," White said, raising his glass.

"And yours."

White drank and set the glass down lightly.

"You saw the colonel yesterday."

"I did." Then Roper realized. "Prince is yours, isn't he?"

White didn't answer.

"You've got your men in the Army," Roper said. "Probably the Navy, too. Captain Morressy thinks the boy is his."

"You saw Morressy, too?"

"You don't know that?" Roper asked. "He came to the hotel, bold as brass, out in the open."

"I told you," White said. "I haven't been watching you."

Roper drank some beer and wiped his mouth on a cloth napkin.

"What'd the colonel want?" White asked.

"He wanted to know what I was doing in Washington," Roper said. "Who I was seeing at Dupont Circle."

"What'd you tell him?"

"That it was confidential."

"Did he buy that?"

"He did."

"He's slipping, you know," White said. "Losing it. But Morressy covers up for him."

"He can't be the only one."

100

"No, he's not," White said. "But nobody really lets him make any important decisions."

"That third bird."

"Yeah, that's it. The third bird."

"Why don't they just give it to him, then?" Roper asked. "Why make him wait?"

"The Army doesn't give anything away," White said. "The word 'give' isn't in their vocabulary. I think that's what's behind this recall of Medals of Honor. They feel they gave away too many of them, which weren't earned." Maxwell the waiter came and set their plates in front of them. White told him to bring two more cold beers.

"Yes, sir."

"These are cooked perfectly," White told Roper.

"You'll see."

And they were, along with the potatoes, onions, and other vegetables.

"So, did you find out about my man?"

"Westover."

"That's right."

"Howard."

Roper stared at White.

"Oddly," the man said, "your man's service record is . . . missing at the moment."

"And you can't find it?" Roper asked. "You?"

"Well . . . there was a fire a few years ago," White said. "Some of the records were lost. His might have been among them."

"How long will it take to find out?"

"I'm not sure."

"And what am I supposed to do in the meantime? I'm sure as hell not going to stay in Washington."

"I'm glad you asked me that." Roper put his knife and fork down and sat back in his chair.

"Why do I have the feeling this free meal is going to cost me more than I could have imagined?"

"Now, just keep eating and hear me out," White said. "We just want you to do a little job for us. It won't even require you to stay in Washington."

Roper eyed the steak. It looked and tasted too good to make it suffer for whatever Donald White was about to say, so he picked up his utensils again.

"All right, damn it," he said to White. "Start talking."

16

"The Army does not want to recall any medals that were well earned," White said.

"That's nice of them."

"So you will need to prove that Howard Westover deserved his medal."

"And how am I supposed to do that?"

"You'll need to get affidavits signed by men who served with him stating he deserved his medal."

"After twenty years?"

"We were around back then, Tal," White said. "A lot of men still are. Just find them and get them to sign."

"How do I know who I'm looking for?" Roper asked. "You can't find his records. You can't tell me where he served, or who he served with."

"No," White said, "but you can get that information."

"From where?"

"From him. He's your client, isn't he?"

Roper hesitated, then said, "Well, not exactly."

"What do you mean?"

"I mean, his wife is my client," Roper explained. "Westover is confined to a wheelchair. He needs to be fed, dressed, changed . . ."

"Can he speak?"

Roper thought back. He'd only heard the man say two words: "Mr. Roper." Did that mean he was lucid? In possession of his faculties? That he'd be able to speak sentences that made sense?

"He can speak . . . I'm just not sure how much sense he'll make."

"Well, find out, man! I'm trying to help you here, Tal. You need those affidavits."

"What about his records?"

"I'll keep looking," White said. "Stay in touch with me. When I find them, I can feed you information that will make your job much more doable."

"Yes," Roper said, "yes, all right. I'll go back and see what I can find out."

"Where is Westover living?"

"West Virginia."

"You can catch the first train tomorrow, be back there in eight hours."

"Why do you want me to leave so soon?"

White dropped his utensils to his plate and

sat back, staring at Roper.

"Aren't you the one who wanted to get out of Washington as soon as you could?" he asked. "Don't get suspicious on me, Tal. I'm telling you how to get this done. You wanted my help, and I'm giving it to you."

"Yes, yes, fine," Roper said.

"Jesus," White said, picking up his fork, "I'm feeding you on Uncle Sam's dime and this is the thanks I get . . ."

"Okay, okay," Roper said. "I'm sorry. This steak is very good."

"Wait until you have their pie."

After their pie — apple for White but cherry for Roper — White paid the bill and they walked outside. Roper was the first to hear the shot. He slammed his shoulder into White's, taking him to the ground. From there he drew his gun and got himself to one knee. He heard someone running toward them and pointed his gun.

"Easy," White said. "That's my driver."

"Are you all right, sir?"

"Yes, I'm fine," White said, "thanks to Mr. Roper."

"Did you see where the shot came from, son?" Roper asked.

"No, sir," the young man said, "I was down the street."

Roper and White got to their feet.

"Come on," White said, giving Roper a push, "let's get to the carriage."

Roper turned around. He noticed that the bullet had missed the windows behind them and instead imbedded itself in the door of the restaurant. Inside, diners had hit the floor, and were now warily getting to their feet.

"Come on!" White said. "Before somebody comes outside and starts asking questions."

The three of them hurried down the street, Roper and the driver with their guns out, keeping White between them. It seemed to be the general consensus of opinion that White had been the intended target.

When they reached the carriage, they climbed in. The young soldier leaped into his seat and got the horse going at a gallop.

Roper holstered his gun and asked, "Does this happen to you a lot?"

"Once in a while."

"So not everyone in Washington thinks you're a bullshit politician."

"Apparently not."

The man on the roof withdrew the rifle and his head, because he knew the men on the ground were the kind of men who would look up first. They'd look for a gunman on a rooftop. He needed to get himself off this roof as soon as possible.

He ran to the back of the roof, dropped down through the open hatch to the floor below. From there he found the back staircase, made his way out the back door to the alley behind the building. He knew he was ahead of the other men. They'd need time — even if it was a matter of seconds — to be sure there wasn't going to be a second shot, before they'd be able to move.

He'd been instructed to take one shot, and one shot only. And miss. It went against the grain for him to miss deliberately, but he was being paid enough to take the sting out of it.

And when he did take a second shot, he sure as hell wouldn't miss.

When they got back to the hotel, the young driver stopped right in front and drew his gun.

"I don't think anyone followed us, Hopkins," White said.

"Can't be too sure, sir."

"Good point," White said. He looked at Roper.

"Well, thanks for an exciting evening," Roper said.

"You know," White said, "I'm not forcing you to leave tomorrow."

"No, you're right," Roper said. "If I'm going to do this, I better get to it. You watch your back."

"And you yours."

Roper climbed down. "I never asked. How long have you been . . . in your current job?"

"Going on five years."

"Do you like it?"

White thought a moment, then said, "I think that comes under the heading of 'Be Careful What You Wish — and Work — For.' "

"Well, good night, then. I'll be in touch when I have something to be in touch about."

"Watch yourself, Tal," White said. "We're not a hundred percent sure that shot was meant for me."

"I'm always careful, Donny."

He went inside to the hotel lobby, approached the desk, and asked the desk clerk to prepare his bill.

"Are you leaving now, sir?"

"First thing in the morning," Roper said. "I'd just like you to have it ready."

"Yes, sir."

Roper went to his room, undressed, sat on the bed, and thought about the evening's events. Considering Donald White's job, someone taking a shot at him was not so unusual by any stretch of the imagination. But someone taking a shot at Roper, in Washington . . . well, that would be too much of a coincidence. Roper would have to assume that it had something to do with his job for the Westovers. But why? Why would someone want to kill him for that? And did it have anything to do with West-over's records being gone?

Roper got his gun from his holster and set it on the night table next to the bed. He thought about reading some more Twain before turning in, then decided against it. He wanted morning to come quickly so he could catch a train and get the hell out of Dodge before somebody else got trigger-happy.

17

Donald White looked up as the door to his office opened. Captain John Morressy walked in.

"How's the colonel?" White asked.

"He's okay. He's back at his residence. And he's being watched."

"You're sure he didn't tell Roper anything?"

"He doesn't know anything," Morressy said, sitting across from the Secret Service head. He took off his hat and rubbed his hand over his short-cropped black hair. "Did he believe your story about the files?"

"Apparently," White said. "Roper is difficult to read, but he seemed to."

"I hope so," Morressy said. "I don't know how smart it is to let him go out on his own."

"He wasn't recruitable," White said. "It has to be done this way. He has to be work-

110

ing for us without knowing he's working for us."

Morressy looked dubious.

"And what happens when he finds out?" he asked.

"I'll deal with that when the time comes."

"You don't think he'll walk away?"

"Not at all," White said. "I know the man. He may not be happy, but once he's involved, he'll see it through."

"You knew him years ago," Morressy said. "How can you be sure he's the same man?"

"Roper doesn't change," White said. "He just becomes more . . . Roper."

"You trust him?"

"With my life."

"But not with the truth?"

"Not yet," White said.

"Why not?"

"Because he's Roper."

Morressy waited, but when there was no more information forthcoming, he stood up, put his hat back on, and turned to the door.

"You took a big chance," White said.

"What?" Morressy turned. "What are you talking about?"

"That shot last night," White said. "You took a big chance."

"What shot?"

"The shot outside the restaurant." White

studied Morressy's puzzled expression. "That wasn't you? Or somebody you sent?"

"No," Morressy said, "I didn't have anyone shoot at you."

White frowned.

"Anybody hurt?"

"No," White said pensively. "There was one shot, and it missed."

"Did they shoot at you or him?" Morressy asked.

"I don't know," White said. "I just assumed you had taken the initiative, thinking it would lock him in."

"I'd never think that."

"Neither would I," White said. "That's why I wasn't happy, but —"

"If it was meant for him," Morressy said, "who knew he was in Washington?"

"I don't know," White said. "The Westover lawyer certainly. What's his name?"

"Harwick."

"Yes, him," White said. "And the Westovers themselves."

"You think they would try to kill him?"

"Why hire him, then try to kill him?" White asked. "No, something else is going on."

"And you feel Roper can unravel this?"

"I know he can."

"How will he react to the shooting?"

"I think he'll be careful," White said, "and assume he was the target. It's the way he'd play it."

"Well," Morressy said, "I just hope you're right about him."

"You and I will stay in touch, Captain," White said.

"Yes, sir," Morressy said, and left.

As the captain left, White sat back in his chair. Of course he was right. After all, it was Talbot Roper. Once he got his teeth into a case, he never let go. That was a trait Donald White thought he could count on, no matter how long it had been since they'd seen each other.

The shot last night, though, that still annoyed him. It seemed clear to him that it had either been meant to kill Roper, or at the very least influence him.

White was used to sending men out to handle danger on their own. They signed up for it when they joined the Secret Service. He was sure Roper could handle any situation that came along, but if the detective ended up dead, White would feel much more guilt than he would if one of his men were killed.

But he'd have to live with it. This was probably the last chance he — and the government — would have to solve a mystery that had existed since the end of the Civil War. And Talbot Roper was going to have to be the man to do it.

18

When Roper returned to Hurricane late the next afternoon, he reclaimed his room. He also asked the clerk to send someone who could deliver a message for him.

"Right away, sir," the clerk said, "and may I say, welcome back."

"Thanks."

He went to his room and freshened up. He was drying his hands when there was a knock at the door. He opened it and let the young bellboy in.

"Take this to Mr. Edward Harwick, either at his home or office. I've written both addresses down." He handed him an envelope with two addresses written on the face. The back was sealed.

He handed the young man a dollar.

"Yes, sir!"

"Let me know as soon as you return and it's done. And tell the dining room I'll be down in ten minutes and would like a table."

"Yes, sir."

The boy left. Roper dressed in fresh, clean clothes, buttoned his jacket over his shoulder holster, and left the room. At that moment all he wanted was a meal.

His table was waiting for him in the dining room.

"Just one, Mr. Roper?"

"Two, I hope," Roper said, "but one for now."

He was shown to a table, where he ordered a steak dinner and a pot of coffee. When his meal came, he ate slowly and went over the plan he'd formed while riding on the train. He had also given the shooting some more thought. White had said he was shot at on occasion. But what if he wasn't the man they were shooting at? What if it was, indeed, Roper? That brought up the question of who and why? Who knew he'd been in Washington, and why would they want to kill him? He knew of only two people who were aware of the trip to Washington — Edward Harwick and Victoria Westover. Unless the two women who worked in the Westover house — Miriam and Polly — listened at keyholes.

He was halfway through his leisurely meal when Edward Harwick entered the dining room. Roper waved, and the man came over and joined him.

"Have you eaten?" Roper asked.

"I was about to when I got your message." A waiter came over, and Harwick ordered the same meal Roper was working on. While Harwick waited for his steak, he poured himself a cup of coffee.

"Did you find out anything interesting in Washington?" he asked.

"I found out quite a bit," Roper said, "but before I tell you, I want to know who you told I was going to Washington."

"What?" Harwick looked startled. "I didn't tell anyone. Why?"

"Because somebody took a shot at me while I was there." He didn't bother to add that he was in the company of the head of the Secret Service.

"What? Were you hurt?"

"No, they missed."

"Well . . . could it have been someone from another case? From your past perhaps? After all, you do have a reputation."

"And they just happened to be in Washington at the same time?" Roper asked. "I seriously doubt it. You told someone I was going."

"No . . ." Harwick started, but then he stopped and said, "The only other person

117

who knew was Victoria."

"Mrs. Westover," Roper said. "Who might she have told?"

"No one."

"You keep saying that, but it can't be true. Somebody knew I was going there — it's that, or one of you had someone shoot at me."

"That's preposterous. Why would we hire you and then try to kill you?"

"That's what I'm wondering. Come on, give it some thought, Harwick."

They paused while the waiter set Harwick's breakfast down in front of him, giving the lawyer some time to think.

"Well," he said when the waiter had left, "there's Howard, but he couldn't tell anyone."

"What about his nurse? Polly?"

"I don't know. I didn't tell her, but I suppose she could have heard Victoria talking to Howard."

"All right," Roper said, "if she knew, who would she tell?"

"I don't know," Harwick said. "She lives there at the house, looks after Howard, and never leaves."

"Never?"

"Well . . . hardly at all."

"Hardly," Roper said. "No one else?"

"No one goes to the house, Roper . . . ever."

"What about Miriam?"

"Miriam?" Harwick said. "She's worked for them for years."

"Does she live in?"

"Well, no —"

"So she comes and goes."

"Yes."

"Is she married?"

"Widowed."

"Does she live with anybody?"

"No. She lives alone. She doesn't have much of a life beyond her work for the Westovers."

"She must go to town, do some shopping? Talk to people?"

"I suppose."

"So someone could have talked with her, maybe gotten the information from her."

"If she knew."

"Believe me," Roper said, "housekeepers, cooks, they know everything that goes on in the houses where they work."

"Well, I'll be going out there again tomorrow," Roper said. "I have things to discuss with the lady of the house. I can also talk to Miriam and Polly."

"Like what you found in Washington?"

"Yes."

Harwick waited, and when Roper didn't speak further, he said, "Well, what did you find?"

"Like I said," Roper responded, "I'll talk with her tomorrow. After that, if she wants to tell you, or wants me to tell you, that's her business."

"But . . . you work for me."

"Mrs. Westover is the client, Edward," Roper said. "Isn't that right?"

19

Roper agreed to ride to the Westover house with Harwick the next morning, even though he continued to refuse to report his findings to him. The lawyer may have fetched him from Denver and gotten him this job, but Roper was being paid by Victoria Westover. His report would be made to her, unless she decreed otherwise.

Harwick pulled up in front of the hotel with his buggy.

"We'll have to be careful," Roper told him, mounting his horse. He had brought his saddle with him on the train, and had left it behind when he went to Washington, but his own horse remained in Denver. This Appaloosa had been rented locally, chosen by him but paid for with Westover funds.

He touched his rifle and then the extra Peacemaker in his saddle holster. So far the razor in his boot had been of little use, but it was always comforting to feel its presence there.

"Careful?" Harwick asked.

"I was shot at in Washington," Roper said. "It could happen here as well."

"Shouldn't we have some protection?" Harwick asked, looking around them. "The law maybe?"

"Don't worry, Edward," Roper said. "I'll protect you."

He kicked the Appaloosa in his painted hindquarters and sprinted ahead. Harwick flicked the reins at his horse and kept up as well as he could.

Before they reached the house, Roper slowed to allow the lawyer to catch up.

"When we get there, I'd like you to let me do all the talking to Victoria," he said.

"Why not?" Harwick asked. "You haven't told me anything anyway."

"Perhaps you'll hear it when she hears it, if she gives me permission to speak in front of you," Roper said. "I also have some questions to ask her that only she may be able to answer."

"I guess we'll find that out when you ask them," Harwick said.

Something occurred to Roper then. "Did you send word ahead that we were coming?"

"No," the lawyer said, "but she'll welcome us. She's been expecting us since the last time we were here."

They stopped in front of the house, secured their horses, and went to the front door.

"Do you have a key?" Roper asked.

"No," Harwick said. "I've not been given that responsibility. We'll knock."

The door was opened by Victoria herself. Roper assumed that the nurse, Polly, the only other person living in the house, never left Howard Westover's side, certainly not to answer the door. The cook, Miriam, wasn't a live-in, but perhaps opening the door was not part of her job.

"Victoria," Harwick said.

"Edward," she said, then looked at Roper. "Mr. Roper, I'm happy to see you back from Washington. I hope you have news for me."

"News," he said, "and questions."

"Come in," she said. "We'll have coffee and pie."

"Sounds good," Roper said, even though he'd just had breakfast. Pie was pie, after all, and not to be turned down.

They went into the dining room and she left them there momentarily to go into the kitchen and then returned empty-handed.

"Miriam is your cook?" he asked.

"Yes," she said, "I'm hopeless in the kitchen."

"Does she live in?"

"No, she goes home in the evenings, after supper."

"I see."

"Is that one of the questions you were talking about?" she asked.

"Yes," he said. "Did you tell Miriam or Polly that I was going to Washington?"

"I did not."

"Could they have found out another way?"

She didn't answer.

"Victoria?"

"I suppose they could have heard us talking," she said. "What is this all about?"

"Somebody tried to kill me in Washington." He didn't tell her there was a fifty-fifty chance the bullet had been meant for someone else.

"I'm sorry to hear that." She didn't look very concerned, though. "Does it have to do with our business?"

"I don't know," he replied. "That's what I'd like to find out."

"I did tell Howard you were going to Washington. He could have told Miriam or Polly."

"I thought he couldn't speak."

"It's a day-to-day thing, depending on his

condition," she said.

"And who might they have told?"

"Polly lives in. She's with him every minute. Miriam goes home, she could have told her brother."

Roper looked at Harwick, who hadn't mentioned a brother. The lawyer shrugged.

"Does he live with her?"

"No, but I assume she sees him."

"And who might he tell?"

"I don't see any reason for him to talk to anyone about it."

"Maybe somebody asked him."

The kitchen door opened and Miriam entered carrying a tray with coffee and pie.

"Perhaps she can answer your questions herself," Victoria said.

"Mum?" Miriam said.

"Mr. Roper has some questions for you, Miriam," Victoria explained. "I'd like you to answer him quite honestly."

Miriam folded her red, thick hands in front of her and asked, "And why would I answer any other way?"

"You're Irish," Roper said, not necessarily in response to her question.

"O'Brien through and through," she said, apparently taking no offense. "Is that one of the questions?"

"Yes."

She stood obediently and waited for the next.

"Did you know I was going to Washington on behalf of your employers?"

"Yes."

"How did you know?"

"I heard you all talking."

"And then did you tell anyone else?"

"No."

"Not your brother?"

"No."

"Why not?"

"I do not discuss my employer's business with anyone," she said, "not even my brother."

"Why not?"

"Because I need my job," she replied. "I have no desire to get fired."

"Did you ever tell Polly about me going to Washington?"

"I don't talk to that one much."

"Why not?"

"I don't like her."

"Why not?"

Miriam sniffed and said, "She's uppity."

Roper looked at the tray. There were three pieces of pie on it, one apple, and two that looked like peach.

"Which pie is better?" he asked.

"My peach is my best pie," Miriam said.

"Then if nobody minds," he said, "I'll have one of the peach slices."

"Of course, Mr. Roper," Victoria said. "Miriam?"

The cook doled out the coffee and served the pie.

"Anything else, mum?"

"Mr. Roper?"

"I have nothing further."

"Not right now, Miriam. Thank you."

The cook nodded, sniffed again in Roper's direction, and went back to the kitchen. He assumed that she did not like him either.

"I didn't mean to insult her."

"She's very proud. Would you like to speak to Polly now?"

"In a while," he said. "Let's eat, and I'll tell you what I found out . . ."

20

"I spoke to someone in the government who has knowledge of the Medal of Honor situation," he told her. He did not reveal Donald White's name, however.

"Are they taking Howard's medal away?"

"That hasn't been decided yet," Roper said. "I asked to look at his war record, but somehow those records are missing."

"What? How could that be? Why?"

"I can't answer any of those questions."

"Then when will the decision be made?"

"I've been given the opportunity to determine if his medal should be taken or not."

"How?"

"I need to speak with some of his colleagues from the war," Roper said. "If I can get some affidavits signed, testifying to the fact that his medal was well earned, it will influence the decision."

"I can probably give you what you need," Victoria said when he'd completed his story.

The pie was also gone, but they were each having a second cup of coffee.

"I need names and locations."

"How many?"

He thought a moment, then said, "Three or four should be enough. Five, to be on the safe side. In case I can't find a couple."

"Or they're dead," Harwick said. It was the first time he'd spoken in some time.

"Good point," Roper said.

"I'll make you a list," Victoria said.

"I'd like to talk to Polly while you do that," Roper said.

"Of course. I'll take you upstairs."

They both looked at the lawyer.

"I'll wait here," he said, waving his hand. "Maybe Miriam can give me another slice of pie."

"Come with me, then," she said to Roper.

In the upstairs hall he asked her again, "How well can your husband speak?"

"Sometimes," she said. "It depends on how well he's breathing."

He remembered the man had said only two words to him when they first met.

"Should I talk to Polly in the hall, or in front of him?"

"In front of him is fine," she said. "If he has something important to say, he'll say it."

Roper nodded.

They stopped in front of a closed door, and he waited for her to open it. When she did, he followed her inside.

Her husband was in bed, lying flat on his back. The nurse, Polly, was standing beside the bed.

"How is he this morning, Polly?" Victoria asked.

"His breathing is labored," the woman said. "I didn't want to risk getting him out of bed."

"All right."

Victoria walked to the bed and put her hand on her husband, over his heart. She kept it there, as if checking to see if he was breathing. Then she turned to the nurse.

"Polly, Mr. Roper has some questions for you," she said. "I'd like you to answer them honestly."

"Of course, ma'am."

"I'll be back in a few minutes," she told both of them, and left.

"Yes, sir?" Polly said to Roper.

"Relax, Polly," Roper said. "You don't have to call me sir."

"I was a nurse in the Army," she said. "It's an old habit."

"Well . . . at ease," he told her.

She smiled but didn't seem to relax much

beyond that.

"Polly, do you know who I am?"

"Well yes, si— yes. You were here only a couple of days ago."

"And do you know where I went after I left here?"

"I understood you were going to Washington."

"Do you know why?"

"I believe it had something to do with Mr. Westover's medal."

"Yes. Polly, did you tell anyone I was going to Washington?"

"No, sir." They were back to that.

"Are you sure?"

"I don't really leave here, Mr. Roper," she said. "Mr. Westover needs constant attention. I don't see very many people."

"No days off?"

"No, sir."

"That's a tough job."

"I understood that when I took the job, Mr. Roper." She looked down at her patient. "I am totally devoted to Mr. Westover."

"I see. So you don't speak to anyone but Mr. and Mrs. Westover, and Miriam?"

Polly smiled. "Miriam doesn't speak to me."

"Why not?"

"She thinks I'm uppity."

131

"Are you?"

"Yes, sir, I am."

Roper liked the woman and believed her. She hadn't spoken to anyone.

"Does Mr. Westover speak to you, Polly?"

"He does, when he can."

"Has he spoken to you about his medal?"

"No."

"Never?"

"Never."

"So when he speaks, what does he talk about?"

"This and that. What he wants to eat, he talks about Mrs. Westover —"

He asked her a question he had never thought to ask the lawyer, or Victoria.

"Do they have any children?"

"No," she said. "They never had children before he went to war, and when he came back, they couldn't. So it has only been the two of them."

"And you and Miriam."

"Yes, sir."

"Okay," he said, "okay. Thank you, Polly."

"Yes, sir."

He looked over at the bed.

"Can he speak today?"

"No," she said, shaking her head. "His breathing is too labored."

"I understand," Roper said. "I'll wait for

Mrs. Westover to return out in the hall."

"Thank you, sir."

Roper nodded and went out. He was at a loss, for the moment, as to who had passed the word that he'd gone to Washington. If, indeed, anyone had. There was still that fifty-fifty chance that the shot had been meant for Donald White. In fact, it would be better for Roper if that was the case. But it seemed he was going to have an itchy spot in the center of his back for the rest of this job.

He turned as a door opened farther down the hall and Victoria stepped out.

"Oh, Mr. Roper," she said. "Would you come in here, please?"

"Of course."

She went in, and he followed, closing the door behind him. He found himself in what was once a bedroom, but was now a room lined with books. There was a writing desk, a wooden chair, and an armchair.

"I spend a lot of time in this room, so that I can be close to Howard," she said. "But I do need my own privacy as well, so it serves a dual purpose."

"I understand."

"Here is a list of names and the last locations I have for them," she said. "These are the men I believe will give you the affirmation that we need."

Roper accepted the list and gave it a cursory glance.

"Victoria, this is going to require quite a bit of travel," he said.

"I understand that."

"It will be expensive."

"I understand that, too," she said. "We can agree on your fee, and then I will cover your travel expenses. I will also have Edward draw up a paper for these gentlemen to sign, legal affidavits that you can take back to Washington."

"That's fine," Roper said. "If he can have those affidavits for me in the morning, I'll get started."

"Very well, then," she said. "If you'll have a seat, we can settle on your fee."

21

Roper rode back to town without Harwick, who stayed behind to discuss the paperwork with Victoria. When he got to town, he returned his horse to the stable, then walked to the nearest bank. He deposited the check Victoria had given him for his fee and an advance on expenses, arranged to have the money transferred to his own bank, and walked out with some cash in his pocket. After that he went back to his hotel to work out a schedule for himself. The men whose names Victoria had given him all lived in points west, so he was going to have to map out a plan of action.

Victoria's handwriting was very flowery, but he could make it out well enough:

Vincent McCord, Saint Joseph, Missouri
Gerald Quinn, Vega, Texas
Henry Wilkins, Jerome, Arizona

David Hampstead, Helena, Montana
Zack Templeton, Pierre, South Dakota

The list had not been written alphabetically, either by name or by state. He stared at it, wondering why she had written it in that order, but then he got it.

It was the perfect order for him to travel. A southerly route across the country, then north.

It made sense.

Now all he needed were the affidavits from Harwick. He folded the paper, put it in his pocket, and went downstairs to find some lunch.

"I think I've got the wording," Harwick said to Victoria.

"Good," she said. "Then you can go back to your office and draw them up."

"Yes."

He stood up. They were in her study, down the hall from her husband's bedroom. He knew that she slept in her own room. He'd never seen it, though he had high hopes.

"I'll walk you out, Edward," she said, taking his arm in both hands.

They went downstairs that way, with her holding on to his arm. He found himself hoping the walk would never end.

When they got to the door, she released his arm. He looked at her. He often wondered if she knew, if she could tell by looking at him, how he felt about her.

"Victoria."

"Yes?"

"Are you sure you want to do this?"

"Yes, Edward," she said, "I'm sure. I know you have your doubts, but I need to make sure Howard doesn't lose his medal. And I need for those men to get what's coming to them. The government couldn't do it, and the law couldn't do it. So I am going to see that it gets done. Can you understand that?"

"Yes, of course."

"I appreciate all your help."

"That's my jo— it's all right. I'll make an extra copy for you to go over."

"That's not necessary," she said, patting him on the arm. "I trust you to do it correctly."

He smiled and said, "I'll bring you one anyway. You can file it."

"Very well."

He stood there a moment, wondering what she would do if he took her into his arms. Would she stiffen and pull away, or would she melt into him?

"All right, then," he said. "I'll get the affidavits to Mr. Roper in the morning."

"Excellent, Edward," she said. "Thank you."

He went out the door, down the stairs, and climbed into his buggy. When he looked back, he thought he might see her standing there, watching him, but she was gone.

Victoria closed the door, feeling sorry for Edward Harwick. She knew he was in love with her. My God, it was written all over his face whenever he looked at her. She wondered if anyone else could tell. Certainly Talbot Roper. After all, he was a detective. He must have been able to see it. Hopefully not Polly and Miriam, though.

She went back upstairs, walked to her husband's room, and entered. Polly was sitting by Howard's bed, reading to him. She did that quite often.

"*Poor Richard's Almanac,*" she said to Victoria, smiling.

"He likes Dickens," Victoria said.

"Yes."

She walked to the bed, put her hand over his heart again. It helped her to feel his chest rising and falling. There were days when he was strong enough to sit up, smile at her, speak to her. Not today, though.

"Polly, I'll be in my study."

"Yes, ma'am."

"I'll see you at supper time." Polly took all her meals in that room, brought to her either by Victoria or Miriam.

"All right."

She left the room, closed the door, and leaned back against it. She wondered if she should have told Talbot Roper more. No, if he was aware of her real plan, he never would have gone along with it. He had a reputation for being a hard, capable man, but also an honest one. There wasn't enough money in the world to corrupt a truly honest man.

22

Roper was having breakfast in the morning when Harwick entered the dining room. He was glad to be leaving Hurricane that morning. He was looking forward to meals in other places, even on the trail. He enjoyed eating over open campfires, and there were a lot of them in his future. Also, after Hurricane and Washington, he found himself longing for open spaces.

"Breakfast?" he asked Harwick.

"No, thank you. I just came to give you these." He held out a large brown envelope.

"Don't be impolite, Edward," Roper said. "At least sit and have some coffee."

"Yes, all right."

"Pour yourself some."

As the lawyer sat and poured, Roper wiped his hands on a cloth napkin, slid the papers out of the envelope, and looked them over. Five single pages, all the same, stating that the signer swears to the fact that the conditions under which Howard Westover earned his Medal of Honor were, in fact, honorable.

He put the papers back into the envelope and set it on the chair next to him, then picked up his utensils again.

"Is that satisfactory?" Harwick asked.

"Thank you, it's fine."

"Will you be leaving today?"

"As soon as I finish my breakfast," Roper said. "I'll keep in contact through telegrams."

"To me?"

"Yes, to you, and to Victoria."

"That's acceptable."

"I'm glad."

The lawyer nodded and started to get up.

"You love her, don't you?"

Harwick stopped, sat back down.

"I wouldn't bother denying it," Roper said. "After all, I'm a detective."

Harwick looked crestfallen.

"Is it that obvious?"

"To me, yes."

"Do you think she knows?"

"Actually," Roper said, "I think she probably does. Women seem to know those things."

Harwick looked across the table, his expression hopeful, as if Roper might have some advice for him on how to handle his feelings.

"So what do I do?"

Roper studied the man for a few moments, then shrugged and said, "Wait it out."

"You mean . . . just wait for her husband to die?" Harwick asked. "That seems . . . I don't know . . . wrong somehow."

"Would it be more right to tell her you love her while her husband's still . . . around?" Roper asked him.

"I don't know," Harwick said, frowning, shaking his head. "Oh, none of this seems right."

"No, I guess not," Roper said, wondering if Harwick was still referring to his feelings for his employer's wife.

Harwick finally stood up.

"I'll await your reports, Mr. Roper."

"I'll send then along, Mr. Harwick."

The lawyer nodded, turned, and left. Roper felt sorry for the man.

Roper arrived at the railroad station minutes before the train was to leave. He handed his saddle to a man in the baggage car, then got on board, carrying his one carpetbag. Most of what he needed for this job he would have to purchase along the way.

142

Some of the trip would be made by rail, the rest of it on horseback. He could rent horses along the way, then return them. Or maybe what he ought to do was buy a good horse and keep it with him when he took the train each time. Horse and saddle could go in the stock car each time. He would have to consider that option.

He found himself a seat, stowed his bag in the compartment overhead, and sat down. The young couple across from him smiled and nodded their heads. They were so young they must have been newlyweds and not experienced travelers. He would not strike up a conversation with them. He preferred to keep to himself when he was traveling for a job. Of course, if they spoke to him, he'd respond politely. So for now he just smiled, nodded back, and then buried his nose in his book. Perhaps, during this train ride, he'd get a chance to finish it.

23

It was days later when Roper rode into the first town on his list, Saint Joseph, Missouri. Best known as the place the pony express had sprung from, Saint Joe had many of the trappings of a modern city, a place in the center of the country where East met West. That meant he saw — as he rode down the main street — a sheriff's office *and* a police station, a saloon *and* a steak house, a general store *and* an apothecary. He was comfortably clad once again in Western clothes, with the gun more comfortably placed on his hip rather than beneath his shoulder.

The first things he needed to find for himself were a livery stable and a hotel, or perhaps a combination of the two, before he started looking for Vincent McCord. When he spotted the Harrison House Hotel, he felt sure he'd found what he was looking for. There was a stable right next to it. He reined in his horse in front of the hotel and dismounted.

When he'd gotten off the train in Saint Louis, he had decided to go ahead and use some of his expense money to buy a horse. He liked the rented Appaloosa he'd ridden in West Virginia, so when he saw one in Saint Louis, he bought it. The animal was small but surefooted. During the three-day ride from Saint Louis to Saint Joe, they had gotten to know each other a bit. Roper knew the animal's idiosyncrasies, and the horse responded well to his touch on the reins.

While he enjoyed eating at a campfire, three days of his own cooking had Roper ready for a good meal. When he walked into the hotel, he was happy to see it had its own dining room.

"Good afternoon, sir," the clerk said. "Just ride into town?"

"Yes, I did. I need a room, and this looked like the best place in town."

"Thank you, sir," the clerk said, "we like to think so." He turned the register book so Roper could check in. "How long will you be staying?"

"I'm not sure. At least a couple of days. I'd like to put my horse up in your livery."

"Of course, sir. I can have that taken care of for you."

"The Appaloosa out front."

"Does he need any special care?"

"Nope, just the usual."

"Yes, sir. Our man is very good with horses."

"That's good to know."

He could have asked the clerk if he knew Vincent McCord, but Roper had learned a long time ago to be cautious when searching for somebody, get the lay of the land before he started tossing a man's name around. Some people didn't like to be found.

The clerk, a middle-aged man with thinning, sandy hair, handed him a key and said, "Room Five, sir."

"Thank you. How long does your dining room serve?"

"Until nine, sir."

"Very good."

"Do you need help with your bags?"

"No," Roper said, "I just have the one, and my saddlebags and rifle. I can manage."

"Very well, sir," the clerk said. "Enjoy your stay."

"Thank you."

Roper went up to the second floor, found Room 5, and let himself in. It was a medium-sized room, clean from the look and smell of it. He dropped his gear on the bed, sat on it, and found it firm enough for his liking. He went to the window, mostly to see what was right outside. The curtains were old, but not threadbare. Satisfied that there was no access to him from that avenue, just a sheer drop, he looked down at the town. The street was busy at midday. There were a couple of buildings across from him that were of the same height, but at the moment nobody with a rifle was taking a bead on him from the roof or a window.

The shot in Washington was still weighing heavily on his mind. There was no good reason for it that he could see. And White's comment that he was shot at "once in a while" didn't ring true. No matter how many times you've been shot at, it's not something you get used to. He wondered if White had sent men to examine the rooftops above.

Roper studied the street but didn't see anyone who looked as if they were paying special attention to the hotel.

Satisfied that he had gone relatively unnoticed, he washed some of the trail dust off, then left the room to go down and see how the food was.

The dining room was midsized, enough tables so that he could not hear the conversations of people sitting across the room.

There was no tablecloth on the table, but the tabletop was clean. The waiter recommended the lamb off the menu. Roper ordered it and found it gamy, but edible. He'd go back to steak next time.

After he finished his meal, he went for a bath and a shave at a place across the street, then stopped in the mercantile and bought a change of clothes. He'd had a suit with him in West Virginia, but left it behind in favor of trail clothes, because of the amount of traveling he was going to be doing. To add to his wardrobe, he bought a shirt and a fresh pair of jeans.

Carrying them wrapped and tied in brown paper, he decided to try the sheriff's office first. Although he had lived in Denver for many years and had been dealing with a police department for much of that time, he still had a Westerner's preference for a sheriff over a policeman. "Sheriff" was an elected position, so people got the man they wanted. Policemen were hired.

He approached the office just as a man appeared, coming from another direction, pushing another man ahead of him, whose hands seemed to be handcuffed behind his back.

"Sheriff," the man whined, "this ain't right."

"Tell it to a judge, Aaron," the other man said. "I warned you about this before."

The cuffed man was wearing an empty holster. The man behind him had an extra gun tucked into his belt, and was wearing a badge.

The sheriff shoved his prisoner face first into the closed door, then reached around him to turn the knob.

"Sheriff?" Roper said.

He had not really meant it as a question, but the lawman took it that way.

"No, I ain't," the man said. "I just do this for fun."

"Sorry," Roper said, "but I need a moment of your time."

"That so? Just get to town, did ya?"

"I did."

"Well, my name's Parnell. Let me get this fella situated in a cell and then we can talk."

"Suits me."

The sheriff opened the door and shoved his prisoner inside. Roper looked around, still conscious of possibly being followed, and then entered the building behind the lawman.

24

The sheriff's office was musty and crowded. It had the pre-requisite desk and stove, some file cabinets and chairs, but everything seemed forced into a space much too small, giving it a cramped feel.

The sheriff shoved his prisoner through a door that presumably led to a cell block. Roper heard the metallic clink of a cell door, and then the man reappeared and tossed a set of keys on his desk.

"Whataya think?" he asked, waving his arms. "They shoved me into this closet when the police department opened."

"Not much room."

"No, it ain't." The sheriff fell into his chair with an audible sigh. He was about fifty, with the air of a much older man. "I'm tired," he said. "Have a seat and tell me your business."

"My name's Talbot Roper," Roper said.

"I'm a private detective working out of Denver."

"Now there's a job," the lawman said. "You're your own boss, ain'tcha? Nobody lookin' over your shoulder. Bet you got a big office, don't ya?"

"Pretty big."

"That's what I should do," the sheriff said. "Set myself up like that. Get much work?"

"I do okay."

"Yeah, I bet," the sheriff said. "So what brings you my way?"

"I'm looking for a man named Vincent McCord."

The lawman's face changed, and he didn't look so relaxed anymore.

"What do you want with McCord?"

There was no reason to lie, so he told the sheriff the truth.

"I want to talk to him about somebody he served with in the war," Roper said. "A man who received the Medal of Honor."

"What's his name?"

"Westover, Howard Westover."

The sheriff thought a moment, then said, "I don't know him." Roper believed him, but there was something on the man's mind.

"So can you tell me where to find McCord?"

"Sure I can," Parnell said. "I can take you

to him if you want."

"I'd appreciate that."

Sheriff Parnell got up and said, "Come on."

They stepped outside, and Roper said, "My horse is at the livery."

"You won't need your horse. We can walk."

He followed the sheriff until he got an uncomfortable feeling about where they were headed.

"There ya go."

Roper had been able to tell minutes earlier that the lawman was walking him to boot hill, just outside of town. Now he looked down at the crudely drawn headstone that simply said VINCE MCCORD.

"What happened?"

"He and his boys got drunk one day and decided they'd like to rob the bank."

"He got shot doing it?"

"No, sir," Parnell said. "They robbed the bank, all right, killed two tellers. One of 'em was a woman. They got away with over twenty thousand."

"So what happened?"

"Posse tracked them down, brought 'em back, and hanged 'em in the center of town. No trial."

"You lead that posse?"

"I wasn't nowhere near the posse," Parnell said. "It was a combination of lawmen and some of the town folks."

"There were lawmen involved in a lynching?"

"They was," Parnell said, "but nobody talks about it. Not ever. The next day this town just went back to business as usual."

"This town's got a pretty good history, what with the pony express and all," Roper said. "That's quite a blemish to have."

"What blemish?" Parnell asked. "I told you, nobody ever talks about it. Why you think this headstone only has a name on it and nothin' else?"

"You mean," Roper asked, "the town goes on as if it never happened?"

"Mister," Parnell said, "as far as this town is concerned, it never did happen. If you go over to the police department right now and ask about the robbery and the hanging, they'll just look at you like you was crazy. There wasn't no robbery, there wasn't no murder, and there wasn't no lynching."

"And you're okay with this?"

Parnell shrugged.

"There ain't a damn thing I can do about it," he said. "Ain't a body in this town would back me if I told that story."

"Then why'd you tell me?"

"Beats me," he said. "I only meant to walk you up here and show you the grave. The rest just come tumblin' outta my big mouth."

"Well, Sheriff," Roper said, "how about we go back to town and I buy you a drink."

"I say that'd be right neighborly of you."

25

Since he was spending the night in Saint Joe, Roper decided to go ahead and get as much information as he could while he was there, so over a beer or two — or four — he asked Sheriff Parnell what kind of man McCord had been. He was interested in the kind of men that had served with Howard Westover in the war. The kind of man Victoria Westover would suggest he contact about her husband's medal.

"McCord was a bad one," Parnell said. "Went to war bad, came back worse. I heard he was almost court-martialed during the war, but it was the eve of a battle and they needed every man they had."

"What happened after the battle?"

"Nothin'," Parnell said. "The officer who was recommending him for court-martial was killed. He just went along fat, dumb, and happy after that, the same man he'd always been."

That certainly didn't sound like the kind of man a Medal of Honor winner would be associated with, but Roper knew you couldn't control who you served with in a war.

"Did anybody else he served with come back here with him?" he asked.

"Nope, just him," Parnell said, "but everybody could see he'd gotten worse. The war gave him a chance to kill, and he developed a taste for it, as well as a taste for cruelty."

"And it took all this time for him to get himself hanged?" Roper asked.

"All what time?"

"Well, it's been over twenty years since the war's been over."

The sheriff looked at Roper strangely, as if the detective were speaking some foreign language, and then seemed to get it.

"Mister," he said, "didn't you notice how old that grave marker was?"

"Well, it was kind of worn," Roper said. "I thought maybe it was used wood they reused over again."

"Naw," Parnell, "wasn't no used wood. That grave's twenty years old."

"What?"

"McCord didn't last very long when he came back to town from the war," the lawman said. "He got himself involved with the wrong people, and ended up at the end of a rope. Where he belonged." The sheriff held out his empty glass. "Another drink?"

Roper went to his hotel after that. He could have checked out and moved on, but it would be dark in a few hours, and that lamb he'd eaten didn't qualify as a good meal to him. He was determined to have a steak before he hit the trail again — even if it was at breakfast.

He tried to read to kill the time — this time with a local newspaper, as he had finished his book on the train — but the things the sheriff had told him about Vincent McCord weighed on his mind. What had possessed Victoria to give him that name? Hadn't her husband talked about McCord when he came home? Hadn't he told her what a bad penny the man was? Why would she think a man like McCord would sign an affidavit to help her husband?

He thought about sending the woman a telegram but decided against it. Instead, he would move on to Vega, Texas, and see what he could find out from the next man on the list, Gerald Quinn. Maybe he'd know something about McCord, and Westover, and any relationship they may have had.

■ ■ ■ ■

He went out to find himself a decent steak dinner a few hours later. There was a different desk clerk on duty, and Roper asked the man where to go if he didn't want to eat in the hotel.

"Down the street, sir, you'll find a place called Thad's. They got right good steaks there."

"Thank you."

Thad's turned out to be a small steak house with two waiters working the floor. One of them showed him to a table with a checkerboard tablecloth and a vase with one rose in the center.

"What can I get you, sir?"

"A steak dinner," Roper said, "all the trimmings, and coffee."

"Comin' up."

As the waiter walked away, Roper saw the sheriff come in the front door. The man spotted him and walked right over.

"I stopped by your hotel and the clerk told me you'd be here."

"What can I do for you?" Roper asked. "Buy you dinner?"

Parnell sat down and considered the question, then smiled and said, "Why not?"

The waiter came with the coffee and Roper told him to bring two steak dinners.

"Comin' up," the man said.

"So what brings you here, other than steak?" Roper asked.

"I remembered somethin'."

"What?"

"McCord had a woman here."

"Before or after he went to war?"

"Both," Parnell said. "She waited for him to get back, and they were together when he got killed."

"Living together?"

"That's right."

"And how do you think this will help me, Sheriff?"

"Well," Parnell said, pouring himself a cup of coffee, "she's still in town. I thought maybe you'd like to talk to her."

Clint studied the man. He didn't know what he could learn from an old girlfriend of Vincent McCord, but he was still in town, so where was the harm in talking to her?

"Will you take me to her?"

"Sure."

"No surprises?" Roper asked. "She's still alive."

The waiter came with their dinners, and as he set them down, Parnell sat back and said, "No surprises."

26

Vincent McCord had lived, at the time of his death, in a small house just walking distance outside of town. It had once been a ranch, but the corral and barn had fallen into disrepair. So had the house, but the smoke from the chimney showed that it was still inhabited.

"What's her name?" Roper asked.

"Tina."

"Tina what? McCord?"

"Naw, she never took his name, but she's used a few different ones. Been married a couple of times."

"What happened to the husbands?"

"They both died."

"Suspicious?"

"Naw," Parnell said, "men just seem to die on Tina."

"Starting with McCord?"

"I guess so."

As they approached the house, Parnell

said, "Let me do the talkin' at first. Tina's been known to answer her door with a rifle. She don't like people."

"She lives alone?"

"Yep, ever since her last husband died a few years ago."

"Okay," Roper said, "whatever you say. You know the lady."

Parnell laughed. "Tina's been called a lot of things, but never a lady."

"Tina!" Parnell called when they got near the house. "Tina, it's Sheriff Parnell!"

The front door opened, and a woman appeared holding a rifle. She was wearing a calico dress that hung on her bony frame. Both the dress and the woman had seen better days.

"Whataya want?"

"Got a fella here wants to talk to you about Vince McCord."

"Why the hell would I wanna talk about Vince?" she demanded. "He's been dead for twenty years. Who is this fella?"

"A detective from Denver," Parnell said. "His name's Roper."

"I never heard of him," Tina said. "Why I gotta talk to him?"

"I'll pay," Roper shouted.

The woman hesitated, then asked, "How much?"

"How much you want?"

More hesitation, then, "Twenty dollars?"

"Done," Roper said, "but I get to come inside."

She thought a moment, then lowered her rifle and said, "Come ahead, both of you."

As they approached the house, she turned and went inside. They followed, closing the door behind them. The musty smell hit Roper first, and the smell of something she'd cooked recently.

"I can make coffee," she said. "It's all I have to offer you."

"That's fine," Roper said.

She came up to him, an angular woman whose angles were more evident this close up. She extended her hand, the dirty palm face up.

"My twenty dollars."

Roper handed it over.

"Sit," she said.

He looked around. In the kitchen area was a pitted old table and a few rickety chairs. Several of the windows had broken panes that had never been repaired. He noticed, however, that the floors were swept clean and there were no spiderwebs anywhere. In her own way, to her own standards, she kept the house clean.

The furniture in the rest of the house — sofa, armchairs, tables — had seen better days, but in their day they had clearly been good stuff. Even her rifle, a Winchester '73, hadn't been cheap in its day.

The two men sat at the table. Roper had his doubts that the chair would hold him, so he sat very still.

Tina put the pot on, and the smell of coffee filled the house. They didn't speak until she had it poured into three chipped mugs and joined them at the table.

"What do you want?" she asked.

"Just some questions about Vincent McCord."

"He was a violent, venal man," she said.

"Then why were you with him?"

"Because a woman needs a man to protect her."

"And now?" Roper asked. "You don't have a man now."

"A young woman needs a man," she said. "A dried-up old woman like me doesn't."

He guessed she was about fifty. Not young, but certainly not an old woman.

"McCord served with several men in the war, one of which was Howard Westover. Do you know that name?"

"No."

"Never heard it?"

"No."

"Did McCord talk about the war?"

"Just some battles," she said. "The killing he did. He thought that would impress me."

"Did he talk about any of the other men he served with?" Roper asked. "Or anything else that he may have done?"

"No," she said, "he only talked about killing."

Roper looked at Parnell, who just shrugged.

"What is it you think he did?" she asked.

"I don't know," Roper said. "I don't know that he did anything. I'm trying to find out."

"Well," she said, "I can't help you. I'm sorry."

They finished their coffee and walked to the door with her. He noticed she picked up her rifle along the way. Obviously, she never went to the door without it.

"Here," he said, pressing another twenty dollars into her hand.

"Our deal was only for twenty," she said.

"That's okay," he said. "It looks like you can use another twenty."

Roper and Parnell walked away from the house. When Roper turned, he saw that she was still standing in the doorway, her rifle in one hand, and twenty dollars in the other.

"That wasn't very helpful," Parnell said.

"Not to me," Roper said. "She did okay, though, don't you think?"

27

He traveled 584 miles to Amarillo, Texas, then stopped there to send a telegram to the lawyer, Harwick, in Hurricane, West Virginia.

He'd decided along the way not to contact Victoria, but to send the lawyer word that he'd found Vincent McCord, long dead, and was on his way to see Gerald Quinn.

Before leaving Hurricane, when he spoke to Victoria the last time, he'd asked her one last question. "Do I have a time limit?"

"My husband is in no imminent danger of dying, Mr. Roper. He is, however, in imminent danger of having his medal stripped from him. Do what you will with that information."

He could have traveled from Saint Joe to Vega by rail — that is, to Amarillo by rail — and then ridden the next thirty miles on horseback. But he decided to ride the entire way. Catching a train meant stopping in the right town, probably staying overnight, checking a rail schedule, catching the next available train — of which there was not necessarily one every day. By the time he did all that, he figured he could be halfway there. He'd bought himself a nice horse, he figured he might as well put the animal to good use.

Roper knew lone riders in the West were fair game. While he slept each night he camped, he slept lightly. Long ago he had discovered his capacity to operate on very little sleep. It had served him well during the war and continued to do so when he was on the trail.

He was also able to exist on very little food — only beef jerky and coffee when he camped. He could carry that in his saddlebags with no trouble. A full packhorse of supplies would only slow him down.

He came to many small towns between Saint Joe, Missouri, and Amarillo, Texas — circumvented most of them, for he had what he needed with him. The only reason to stop in one of these small towns would be to restock, which he expected to have to do only once before he reached his destination.

He chose a town called Los Lunas, New Mexico, in which to make his stop.

The shot in Washington still played on his mind. If he'd taken the rail route to Amarillo, he would have made a stationary target. On the trail he was a moving target. But stopping in a town, once again he'd be stationary. So he intended to stop only as long as it took to buy more jerky, coffee, and maybe some beans this time.

Los Lunas was a smudge, a one-road town with half a dozen buildings that had seen better days, which included a saloon and a mercantile, but no jail. Most likely there was no law around.

He rode his Appaloosa up to the trading post and dismounted. He could have used a drink, but stopping in a saloon was as good as looking for trouble, especially in a hole like this.

He looped the horse's reins around a hitching post and entered the store. Shelves on all sides were piled high with supplies. He was surprised at how well stocked it was for such a small town. There were probably ranches in the area that did all their restocking here.

The man behind the wooden counter said, "Welcome, stranger, welcome to Sandusky's. That's me. I've got everything you need here, best-stocked store for miles. Just tell me what you need, and if you have

168

the money to pay for it, it's yours."

He was tall, red-haired, and pale, looked to be about sixty. His clothes looked handmade, and Roper suspected he had a wife or daughter who had made them. His hands showed the signs of years of hard work, some of the fingers bent, many of the nails broken.

Roper approached the counter, a sheet of wood that had been sandpapered smooth.

"Coffee, jerky, and beans."

"Is that all?"

"No," Roper said. "A box of 'forty-five shells."

"Comin' up."

The merchant collected the items and brought them to the counter. He wrote out a bill and handed it to Roper.

"Can I wrap these items in brown paper?" Sandusky asked.

"No, just put them in a small sack," Roper said. "I'll be putting them in my saddlebags."

"Sure you don't need anything else?" the merchant asked. "A new hat? New boots?"

"My hat and boots are fine, thanks."

"Suit yerself," Sandusky said. "You ain't gonna find another store like this between here and Amarillo."

"Okay," Roper said, "I'll take one more thing."

"What's that?"

Roper pointed to an item on the shelf behind the man.

"Ah," the man said, taking a bottle down, "the finest Tennessee sippin' whiskey."

"Add it to the bill."

Sandusky did as he was told, and Roper paid the total. The merchant put everything into a sack and handed it to Roper.

"Thank you."

"Stayin' in town?" Sandusky asked.

"No, I just stopped for some supplies. I'll be on my way."

"Well, then, I have to warn you."

"About what?"

"The Castles."

"There are castles near here?" Roper asked.

"No, no," Sandusky said, "the Castles are three brothers who live here. They . . . usually try to rob my customers when they leave here."

"Do they usually succeed?"

"Oh, yes," the man said. "I'm sorry I didn't tell you before you paid, but —"

"That's okay," Roper said. "I've dealt with highwaymen before."

"Yes," Sandusky said, "you strike me as

170

the kind of man who has."

"I'm assuming there's no law in this town?"

"Not for a very long time," Sandusky said. "You'll be able to do whatever you need to do when you leave here."

"Can you tell me anything else about the Castles?"

"Three brothers," Sandusky said, "who are very used to getting what they want with no resistance."

"Thank you," Roper said. "That's exactly what I needed to know."

He took his sack, turned, and left the store, hoping for the best, but expecting the worst.

28

As he stepped outside, Roper saw the three men standing in the street. One was next to his horse, with his hand on the animal's rump. They were all the same, over six feet, wearing threadbare clothes and with old but lethal pistols in their belts. None wore a hat, and all had the same unruly black hair. He could say that they were of differing ages, but definitely brothers. The one with his hand on the Appaloosa's rump looked to be the oldest. As it turned out, he was the spokesman.

"Hello, friend," the man said.

"Hello."

"Don't seem like you bought very much in the way of supplies."

"I didn't need very much."

"Sandusky's usually a pretty good salesman," the man said.

"He did convince me to buy a bottle of whiskey."

"Whiskey!" one of the other men said. He wiped his hands with his fingers.

"Shut up!" the older one said.

"Are you the Castle boys?" Roper asked.

"We are," the older one said. "I'm Lem, that's Cal and Bill. Sandusky tell you that?"

"Well . . ."

"He warned you about us, didn't he?" Lem asked. "That wasn't real smart of him." Lem looked at his brothers. "We're gonna have to teach Sandusky a lesson when we're finished here."

Roper realized he'd made a mistake, and he'd trapped himself so that he had only one out. If he managed to leave here with his supplies, without killing these men, Sandusky would no doubt pay the price.

"Nice horse," Lem said. "I think I'll start with this."

"Start what?" Roper asked.

"Me and my brothers, we get to pick what we're gonna keep. I'm gonna keep the horse."

"I want his gun," Bill said.

"I want that bottle of whiskey," Cal said.

"I'm afraid you boys are shit out of luck," Roper said. "You can't have any of those things."

"Now look," Lem said, "if Sandusky warned you about us, he told you why. So it

173

ain't too smart of you to refuse. You might as well start walkin' now."

"I don't intend to walk anywhere," Roper said. "And I'll advise you to take your hand off my horse."

"My horse," Lem said. "And those are my supplies you're holding."

"No," Roper said. "It's all mine. Step aside, and I'll be on my way."

Lem dropped his hand from the horse's rump, and his two brothers tensed.

"There's three of us," Lem said. "You ain't got a chance."

"But I intend to resist," Roper said. "Sandusky said you're not used to that. Are my horse and what I have in this sack worth dying for?"

"Ain't us is gonna die, friend," Lem said. But his brothers didn't seem as sure. They were used to scaring people and meeting no resistance. This obstinacy was new to them.

Roper remained on the boardwalk in front of the store. It gave him an advantage, looking down on his three opponents. They were sufficiently spread out, though, to give him trouble. If he could just get them to stand closer together . . .

"Your brothers don't look so confident, Lem," Roper said. "You better talk to them."

Lem turned and looked at his brothers,

then back at Roper.

"Don't you worry, my brothers will do what they have to do," he said, but he did move away from the horse, toward his brothers.

"Okay, boys," Roper said. "Let's get this over with. Either I mount up and ride out, or you go for those guns in your belts and hope they don't blow up in your hands."

"What's he mean?" Cal asked his brother.

"Have you boys ever even fired those guns?" Roper asked.

Bill looked down at the gun in his belt, frowning.

"Never mind," Lem said. "That's enough talk. Start walkin' or pay the price."

"I already paid in there," Roper said, jerking his thumb at the store behind him. "Out here, you're the ones who will pay."

"There's three of us," Lem said again.

"But you're just three bullies, used to getting your way," Roper said. "I'm a professional. You don't stand a chance."

"Goddamn you —" Lem said, and reached for his gun.

Roper knew that speed was revered when it came to gunplay, but it was accuracy that kept men alive. He calmly drew his gun and fired, first at Lem, because he was the most dangerous.

He'd been right about the three brothers. Beating men with their fists came easy to them. Gunplay did not. Lem had to grab for his gun twice, and by then Roper's bullet struck him in the chest, knocking him backward and then onto his back in the street.

Cal grabbed for his gun, but only managed to pull the trigger while it was still in his belt. He shot himself in the leg just moments before Roper shot him in the belly.

Roper turned his attention to Bill last. The younger brother pulled his gun free of his belt, but as he tried to bring it to bear, Roper shot him in the hip. The bullet spun him around just at the same time he was pulling the trigger. The old gun exploded in his hand, and it was the backlash from that explosion that killed him in the end, not Roper.

When the shooting had stopped, Sandusky came out of his store to survey the results.

"Well, thank God," he said.

Roper turned to look at him, then stepped into the street. He walked to the three brothers to determine that they were all dead. He still held his sack of supplies in his left hand.

His horse had shied from the gunfire but, tied fast, had been unable to run off. Roper walked to him now and patted his neck, speaking to him softly. Then he looked at Sandusky.

"Thanks for the warning, Sandusky."

"Don't thank me," Sandusky said. "Every time I have a customer who looks like he can handle himself, I give him the same warning. You're the first one who's been able to do anything about it. So I thank you. Now my customers won't have to worry about being robbed."

"Glad I could help," Roper said. He ejected the spent shells from his gun, reloaded, and then holstered it. "I'll be on my way."

Roper transferred the supplies from the sack to his saddlebags, then mounted up. He waved at Sandusky and rode out of Los Lunas. Just outside of town he took the bottle of whiskey from the saddlebags, uncapped it, and took a long pull. He'd killed men before, for good reasons and for bad, and it was never easy to deal with afterward. He always found the before easier. Even while he was using his gun, firing lead into men's bodies, it was easier. It was the aftermath that weighed heavily on him — even during the war. He took another swig from the bottle and then replaced it in his saddlebag. Then he continued riding toward Amarillo, hoping he wouldn't have to stop again until he got there.

29

Talbot Roper rode into Amarillo about eleven days or so after leaving Saint Joe. He'd stopped to restock only that one time in Los Lunas, carrying with him only enough supplies to see him through until the end of his journey. The one thing Roper did on every job he took was keep himself mobile, able to move at a moment's notice without worry of leaving anything behind. Guns, horse, and saddle were enough. The rest he could replace later.

In Amarillo he reined in the Appaloosa in front of the telegraph office, went inside, and carefully worded a message to the lawyer to report his progress.

He came out of the telegraph office, untied his horse, and walked it across the street. He tied it off again in front of a saloon and went inside. One beer to cut the dust and he'd be on his way.

He trusted himself to avoid trouble in Amarillo, as he had failed to do in Los Lunas. For one thing, Amarillo had plenty of law. And the people had more to do with their time than hang around outside the mercantile or general store to rob people.

"Help ya?" the bartender asked.

"Cold beer," Roper said.

"Comin' up."

The saloon was called The Bent Tree, and hanging over the mirror behind the bar was a huge bent tree limb. The bar was about twelve feet long, made of varnished and polished wood, with plenty of tables on the floor, some of which were set up for faro or poker.

Roper accepted his beer, paid for it, then turned and drank it while leaning against the bar. The cold beer cut the dust that coated his throat and spread a wonderful cool feeling through his belly.

It was midday, and only about half the tables were occupied. The gaming tables were not yet up and running. There was one saloon girl working the floor, but he knew by that evening there'd be three or four.

He nursed his beer, gratefully swallowed the last bit of it, then set the empty mug on the bar.

" 'Nother?" the bartender asked.

"No, thanks. One was all I needed."

"Stayin' in town or passin' through?"

"Passing through," Roper said. "I'm on my way out right now."

"Good luck to you, then."

"Thanks."

He came out and found a boy looking at his horse.

"What do you think?" he asked.

The boy turned his head and looked at him. He was about ten years old, had a dirty face, a blond cowlick, and brown eyes.

"Nice horse."

"Yeah, he is."

"Does he have a name?"

"No."

"You ain't named him?" The boy closed one eye quizzically.

"No."

"Why not?"

"Haven't had time really."

The boy looked at the horse, then at Roper again. "For two bits I'll name him for ya."

"Two bits?" Roper asked. "That's kind of steep for a name, isn't it?"

The boy bit his lip and thought a moment.

"How about a nickel?"

"I think I could do a nickel," Roper said. "But it better be a good name."

The boy stared at the horse again, gave it some serious, brow-furrowing thought, then brightened and said, "How about Nickel?"

"And if I had agreed to two bits," he asked, "would you have said Two-Bits?"

"Yeah."

"You're a very enterprising young man," Roper said.

The boy put out a grimy hand and said, "A nickel, please."

Roper took out two bits and put it in the boy's hand.

"Wow."

"Okay, Nickel," Roper said to the horse, freeing the reins from the hitching post, "let's go. On to Vega."

"You goin' ta Vega?" the boy asked.

Roper mounted up and stared down at the boy.

"Yes, I am."

"For two bits I'll tell you somethin' about Vega."

"Do you really know something about Vega?"

The boy nodded his head.

"Okay." Roper took out another two bits and tossed it to the boy, who caught it in the air very nimbly.

"Okay," Roper said. "Talk."

"Ain't nothin' there."

Roper waited, then asked, "That's it?"

"That's what my pa says," the boy answered. "He don't know why anybody would go to Vega. There ain't nothin' there."

"What's your name, boy?"

"Jackson."

"Thanks, Jackson," Roper said. "Don't spend it all on candy."

Roper wheeled his horse around and headed out of town, knowing that the minute he turned, the boy was off to spend every penny on candy.

And why not?

30

He made Vega before nightfall. Jackson's pa had almost been right. There was almost nothing there, just a few buildings. One of them, however, was a saloon. He reined in his horse in front of it and dismounted. He looped the reins over a rail, said, "Wait here, Nickel," and went inside.

He stopped just inside the batwings, looked around. There were about ten men in the place, plus the bartender. They all stopped what they were doing — drinking, talking — and looked at him. He looked back, then walked slowly to the bar.

"Lost?" the bartender asked.

"Why do you ask?"

"Nobody ever comes here unless they're lost."

"How about to have a beer?"

"Is that what you want? A beer?"

"Yes."

"Comin' up."

He drew a beer from the tap and carried it over to Roper.

"Four bits."

"Twice as much as a horse's name."

"What?"

"Never mind. Thanks."

The bartender nodded. He was a big man with thick hands, sloping shoulders, the kind of man who broke up bar fights with those hands.

"How many people live in this town?"

"Not sure."

"Let me ask you this," Roper said. "Does everyone who's in here now live here?"

"Yeah."

"But there are more?"

"Oh, sure," he said. "Why are you askin'?"

"I'm looking for someone."

"Are you law?"

"Do you have any law here?"

From underneath the bar the bartender took out a badge and set it on top.

"Is that yours, or are you offering it to me?"

"It's mine, I guess," he said with a shrug. "Nobody else wants it."

"Then you're the man who can help me."

"That depends."

"On what?"

"On whether or not you're looking for

trouble," the bartender/sheriff said. "And you ain't answered my question. Are you any kind of law?"

"I'm no kind of law, Sheriff."

"Don't call me that." He took the badge off the top of the bar, stowed it back underneath. "My name's Dan."

"Okay, Dan. My name's Talbot Roper, I'm a private detective from Denver."

"Denver. What are you doin' here?"

"I'm looking for a man named Gerald Quinn."

Dan didn't say anything.

"Is he in here? One of these?"

"No," Dan said.

"Do you know him?"

"Yeah," Dan said, "yeah, I know him."

"Can you take me to him?" Roper asked. "Or tell me where he is?"

"What for? What do you want Quinn for?"

"I want to talk to him about a man he served in the war with," Roper said. "A Medal of Honor winner."

"Is that a fact?"

"Yeah, it is."

Dan didn't answer.

"I just want to ask him some questions," Roper said.

"Are you plannin' on payin' him?"

"No, I wasn't," Roper said. "But I suppose I could."

"How much?"

"I could negotiate that with him."

The bartender/sheriff did some thinking.
Roper sipped his beer.

Finally he asked the man, "Do you want
me to pay you?"

"No," Dan said, "I don't need your
money, Roper. But Quinn does."

"Fine," Roper said. "I'll pay him something."

"Okay," Dan said. "Okay, I'll take you to
him."

"Good."

Dan looked around the room, then said,
"Hey, Harry."

"Yeah?"

He came around the bar.

"Watch the place for me for a while. I
gotta go out."

"I get a free beer?"

"Yeah, have a free beer." Dan looked at
Roper. "Follow me."

Outside he said to Roper, "As soon as
we're gone, he'll give everybody a free beer."

"I'll pay," Roper said.

"This way," Dan said. "You won't need
your horse."

"You're not taking me to a grave site, are
you?"

31

Dan led Roper to a dilapidated house just outside of Vega. Everything around it was dead or dying. All hardscrabble ground, dead brush and trees. Dead, like the town.

"Quinn lives there."

"Alone?"

"Yeah."

"It's quiet."

"Yeah," Dan said. "Too quiet."

"I'm going to go in," Roper said, drawing his gun.

"Yeah, okay."

Roper approached the house carefully, listening intently for any movement. When he got to the door, he saw that it was flimsy and ajar. Wouldn't have taken much to force it.

He pushed the door open with his elbow, went inside holding his gun in both hands out ahead of him.

"Quinn?" he said.

Nothing.

"Gerald Quinn?"

Still no answer.

There was a second room. Roper went to the door, pushed it open with his foot, then stepped inside. That's where he found Gerald Quinn — or a man he assumed was Quinn — shot in the back. He'd need the bartender, Dan, to make sure.

He checked the body first. The man had been shot twice. The body was still warm, the blood fresh. He turned and went to the front door, waved Dan in.

"What is it?" the man asked.

"In there."

Dan went to the back room and looked inside, then turned and looked at Roper.

"Is that Quinn?" Roper asked.

"Yeah," Dan said. "Did you kill him?"

"No," Roper said.

He'd holstered his gun. Dan came out from behind his back with one and pointed it at him. Roper had seen the man secrete the gun behind his back in the bar. He'd wondered when it would make an appearance.

"How do I know you didn't kill him?"

"He's been shot twice," Roper said. "Did you hear any shots?"

"How do I know you didn't kill him an

hour ago?"

"Why would I kill him, and then come into the saloon looking for him?"

"So nobody would think you killed him."

"If I killed him, why didn't I just ride away?"

Dan studied Roper, then said, "I ain't no good at bein' a lawman."

"Relax," Roper said. "Put the gun away."

Dan looked at the gun in his hand as if he were seeing it for the first time. "Oh, sorry." He stuck it in his belt.

"Anybody around here want Quinn dead?"

"Nobody around here wants nobody dead," Dan said. "We're all just tryin' ta survive."

This was too much of a coincidence, the first two men on his list being dead. Even though the first had been dead over twenty years. Roper had a most uncomfortable feeling.

"Why don't we go back to the saloon," he said, "and you can arrange a burial detail."

"Bury him that fast?" Dan asked. "Somebody's gotta find out who killed him."

"Well, if you're the sheriff, it's your job."

"I ain't no sheriff," Dan said. "I'm a barkeep. I'm just holdin' on to the badge. How about you? You wanna be sheriff?"

"Of Vega? No thanks. I've already got a job."

"Well, whatever your job is, you was lookin' for Quinn. Can you find out who killed him?"

"You know, Dan," Roper said, "I think I probably could."

The man called Kilkenny watched them from behind a tree. He knew Roper wouldn't be far behind him, but this had been close. Quinn's blood was still wet on the floor.

He waited while they discovered the body, then watched as they walked back to town. He knew they'd be coming back with somebody to collect the body. It would have been easy to pick Roper off, just as easy as it would have been in Washington. But he'd missed on purpose then, and he had no orders to fire any more shots at the detective. When he did fire next, it would be for real.

As soon as they were gone, he came out of hiding, then walked to where he had hidden his horse. Before mounting up, he took the list from his pocket, and a nub of a pencil, leaned against the leather saddle, and drew a line through Quinn's name.

That left Wilkins, Hampstead, and Templeton.

He put the list away and mounted his horse.

They walked back to the saloon, where Dan announced that Gerald Quinn was dead. That seemed to upset everyone. Vega appeared to be a close-knit community, and they didn't take it well that one of their number had been killed.

"This guy do it?" one of them asked.

"No, he found the body with me. Quinn was shot twice, and this fella ain't fired a shot."

"Then who did it?" somebody else asked.

"I dunno."

"Do you?" Roper was asked.

"No," he said, "but I just might be able to find out."

"How?"

"By continuing on with my job," Roper said. "If somebody killed him because they didn't want me talking to him, I'll find out. Meanwhile, you might want to call in the law from Amarillo. Or maybe somebody federal, like a marshal."

"And what will you be doin'?" Dan asked.

"I still have a few more men to find and

talk to," Roper told him. "That is, unless they're all dead already."

32

Roper stopped at the next town that had a hotel and got himself a room. He counted himself lucky that the citizens of Vega had let him leave. They could have held him until they got a proper lawman on the job. As it was, he'd left his name, and when a sheriff or marshal did arrive, he was going to be damned angry that they'd let him go.

Roper only intended to stay the night. He needed some time to figure out his next move. The next name on his list was Henry Wilkins in Jerome, Arizona. After that David Hampstead, in Helena, Montana, and Zack Templeton in Pierre, South Dakota.

But what if he got to Jerome and found Wilkins dead? Freshly killed? That would definitely mean that someone was either following him, or working off the same list he was, in the same order. Why would that be? Who would have given them the same list he'd gotten from Victoria?

Somebody was lying to him. Victoria? Harwick? Donald White?

If he was being used, he could spoil the plans by forgetting everything and going back to Denver. But if he did that, and three more men died, how would he feel?

He could send each of the three men a warning telegram and *then* go home. Or send them a telegram and continue on.

But if he wasn't going to go home, why should he continue on in the original order? Why not mix it up?

He was getting a headache, and he was hungry. He decided to continue his thought process over a meal, and then a drink.

The town was called Shamrock, the hotel the Shamrock Hotel, and the saloon the Shamrock Saloon. Whoever had founded the town had remarkably little imagination.

He went to a restaurant called O'Malley's and, in keeping with everything else in town, ordered Irish stew.

"Our specialty," the proud waiter said.

"And a mug of beer."

"But of course."

The waiter brought the beer, and minutes later a steaming bowl of stew.

"Enjoy your meal, sir."

"Thank you."

By the time Roper finished his meal, he had decided to move on to Arizona to find Henry Wilkins. It was just so much closer than Montana or South Dakota. But he'd also decided to send a telegram ahead, warning the man that he was in danger. And he was going to take steps to make sure he wasn't followed. If someone tried to kill Wilkins before he arrived in Jerome, Arizona, it would mean that someone was ahead of him, not following him. That would mean they were working off the same list. If that was the case, he'd send telegrams to the other two men, and to Harwick and Victoria in West Virginia, telling them he was done, because at that point it would be obvious that he had not been told everything.

And then there was the involvement of Donald White. If it was anyone else, Roper would think he was being set up as a patsy, but maybe he was actually being set up as a bird dog. His friendship with White notwithstanding, there had to be some Secret Service duplicity going on here.

He walked back to his hotel, mindful of whether or not he was being watched. If he was, it was by somebody who knew what he was doing. Somebody with training.

He spent a fitful night and got an early start the next morning.

33

Roper did his best to lose anyone that was following him when he left Shamrock, Texas, and then instead of riding the six hundred miles to Flagstaff, Arizona, he made the trip by rail.

Flagstaff was the largest town near Jerome, about eighty miles away. Sedona was between the two, but he wasn't sure what Sedona was like these days. Flagstaff, on the other hand, had grown by leaps and bounds.

He got off the train at the Flagstaff station, retrieved his horse and saddle from the stock car, then got the horse situated at a livery stable. Again he got himself a hotel room, just for the night. In the morning he'd head for Jerome, but before he did, he had some telegrams to send.

He left the Carriage House Hotel after getting his room and walked to the telegraph office. All during the trip he had been carefully wording the telegrams, and he wrote them out exactly that way.

He intended to send one to Jerome, to Henry Wilkins, warning him that his life might be in danger and he should take steps to protect himself until Roper arrived. He didn't know how Wilkins would react, but if Roper himself got a telegram like that, he'd get real careful. That was all he wanted from Wilkins.

"There ain't a telegraph key in Jerome," the key operator told him.

"Where's the closest one?"

"Sedona."

"Okay, send it to Sedona with a request that someone get it to Henry Wilkins in Jerome."

"Okay."

The next one went to Harwick, in West Virginia. This one said he couldn't locate Quinn, but was on his way to Helena, Montana, to see David Hampstead. He also asked Harwick to pass the word to Victoria. They'd probably wonder why he'd go from Texas to Montana without stopping in Arizona, but let them wonder.

He couldn't send a telegram to Donald White in Washington. You can't just send the head of the United States Secret Service a telegram. But if White had somebody keeping an eye on Harwick and Victoria,

199

he'd know what the telegram said. Hopefully, he'd be confused as well.

Roper wanted everyone but himself confused.

He kept a low profile in Flagstaff, kept an eye out his window for someone trailing him, ate in the hotel, and left early the next morning for Sedona. If he pushed, he could probably make it by nightfall, but that would tax the horse to his limit. He decided to make the ride in two days, and keep a sharp eye behind him.

In Hurricane, West Virginia, Edward Harwick took Roper's telegram with him to the Westover home and showed it to Victoria.

"I don't understand," she said. "He doesn't say why he couldn't find Quinn, or why he'd go to Montana from Texas when Arizona is closer."

"I don't understand either."

"Are we sure Mr. Roper knows what he's doing?"

"He has an impeccable reputation and many good references."

She sighed heavily and said, "Then I guess we just have to trust he has his reasons."

"That's what I suggest," Harwick said.

"Thank you for bringing this to me,

Edward. Stay to dinner?"

He smiled and said, "Of course."

In Washington, D. C., a man entered Donald White's office and handed him a piece of paper.

"When was this delivered?" he asked.

"Today, sir, to Hurricane, West Virginia."

"Okay, thank you. You can go."

"Yessir."

After the young man left, White unfolded the message and read it.

"What the hell is he up to?" he asked himself.

34

Roper rode into Sedona the next afternoon with a few hours of daylight left. Jerome was another twenty miles, and he wasn't sure whether he should rest the horse or push him.

He stopped in front of a saloon, decided to consider the matter over a beer. Ten minutes, he told himself, he had to make up his mind in ten minutes.

The saloon was busy, but he was able to make a space for himself at the bar. He ordered a beer and drank half of it down gratefully. He still wasn't sure he was doing the right thing. Whoever was behind the killing, whoever was trying to pull strings here, he'd cross them up completely if he just went back to Denver. But then he'd be wondering about the last three names on the list, and whether they were dead or alive — even if he sent telegrams warning all of them.

A scuffle started at the end of the bar, and the chain reaction from it caused the guy next to him to bump Roper and spill some beer on him. His own beer, half done, was safe.

"Jesus, I'm sorry, friend," the man said.

"That's okay," Roper said. "No problem."

"Those asses at the end of the bar —"

"It's fine."

"Lemme buy you another beer."

"It's okay," Roper said. "You didn't spill any of mine."

"I insist," the man said, and waved at the bartender to bring two more drinks.

"Thank you," Roper said when the man handed him the second beer. He quickly finished the first one and set the mug down, then switched the beer to his left hand so that his gun hand would be free.

"Just get to town?" the man asked.

"Yes, just about ten minutes ago."

"Sedona's a nice town," the man said. "You lookin' for work?"

"No."

" 'Cause I'm hirin' for my boss, out at the Double-B," the man went on.

"I've got a job, thanks."

"Oh? Whataya do?"

Roper didn't answer.

"Hey, I'm sorry," the man said. "I ask a

lot of questions. You probably don't even wanna talk about your work."

"As a matter of fact, I don't."

"Say no more," the man said. "Enjoy your beer."

"Thanks."

The man finished his beer and left the saloon. Roper was glad. He wasn't looking to make any new friends.

As the man who bought him the beer left, so did two other men. Roper watched them leave, and thought they were paying him some undue attention. He had a feeling that buying him the beer had been a signal of some kind. These were, after all, the two men who had started the shoving match at the end of the bar.

He called the bartender over.

"Who was that fella that was standing here with me?"

"I don't know," the bartender said. "Never saw him before."

"He doesn't work on a ranch near here?"

"Not that I know of," he said, "and I know all the hands around here."

"Okay, thanks."

"Sure."

"Is there another way out of here?"

"Not for the public."

Roper put a dollar on the bar.

"Back door, behind the stage."

The stage was small and, at the moment, empty. Roper walked across the room, went through the door, and walked down a hallway to a back door. He went out the door, looked both ways. There were alleys on either side of the building. He chose the right side, turned down the alley, and took it to the main street.

At the mouth of the alley he stopped and peered out. Sure enough, the fellow who'd bought him the beer was waiting across the street, and on either side of him were the other two men. They were waiting for him to come out the front door.

He had choices. He could go the other way, but his horse was in front of the saloon. He could go looking for a lawman for help, but that went against his grain on solving his own problems. Besides, he needed to know if these men had anything to do with the death of Gerald Quinn in Vega. He needed to find out if they had followed him to Sedona.

He made up his mind. He did go the other way, but only for a block, then he crossed over so that he was on their side.

They were fairly relaxed, probably certain that he was coming out the front door and

would be a sitting duck for them.
Who was the sitting duck now?

35

The three men were watching the front door, not looking from side to side at all. It was fairly easy for Roper to move up close to them, about two doors down. It was as close as he wanted to be.

People walking by noticed him and suddenly decided to cross the street. Before long everybody noticed something was going on and started crossing the street. Eventually, the three men noticed the exodus to the other side, and looked around.

"Hello, boys," Roper said. "Sorry to disappoint you, but I didn't use the front door."

As they turned to face him, they were standing single file, which meant two of them did not have a clear shot. Besides, Roper already had his gun in his hand, although it wasn't pointed at them.

"No, don't move," he told them. "I like you the way you are. I could probably take all three of you with one bullet."

"W-What are you talking about?" the man who'd bought him the drink asked.

"I need to know what's going on here," Roper said. "Did you follow me here from Flagstaff? Or did you just pick me out when I entered the saloon?"

"We don't know what you're talkin' about, friend," the man said. "All I did was buy you a drink."

"Look, the three of you were out here waiting to bushwhack me. That kinda makes me mad. I'm going to give you one chance." He pointed his gun at them. "Go for your guns."

One of the other men said, "You're crazy. You already have your gun pointed at us."

"My way of equaling the odds," Roper said. "You don't like it?"

"I don't like it," the third man said.

"Me neither," said the second man.

"Fine," Roper said. "Walk away."

The two men did not waste any time. They stepped into the street, then hurriedly turned and rushed the other way.

The remaining man went to step in the street and Roper said, "Not you, friend."

"Hey, l-look, friend, all I did was buy you a beer."

"I want to know," Roper said, "did you follow me, or pick me out in the saloon?"

"I — I don't know what you're talkin' about," the man said. "I didn't follow you from nowhere. Anybody can tell you I been in this town for a month."

"So you just figured when I walked into the saloon, I was easy pickings?"

"Well . . . yeah."

"You picked the wrong man."

"Yessir."

"You were going to kill me," Roper said. "You think I should let you walk away for that?"

"Y-You let them walk away."

"They were flunkies," Roper said. "You're the head man."

"I ain't no head man," the man said. "You just came and stood next to me."

"Just coincidence, huh?"

"Y-Yessir."

Roper still wasn't sure, and he didn't want to let this man go until he was.

"What's your name?"

"Stark."

"Okay, Stark, where's your horse?"

"I-In front of the saloon."

"Walk to it."

Stark started to step into the street.

"First drop your gun. Take it out careful like, with two fingers."

He stopped, took his gun from his holster,

and dropped it to the ground.

"Okay, let's go," Roper said, "and if I find anything in your saddlebags that makes me think you followed me, I'm going to kill you, so tell me now if White sent you, or if you came from West Virginia."

"West Virginia?" the man said. "I ain't never been to West Virginia. And who's White?"

"If you're acting, you're doing a good job," Roper told him.

"Mister, I'm tellin' you the truth. I'm just a plumb terrible actor."

"We're going to see," Roper said. "Which horse is yours?"

"Th-The mare next to the Appaloosa."

"Walk to it, my friend," Roper said. "The next few minutes are very important to you."

36

When they reached the horses, Roper said to Stark, "Empty it all out."

"What?"

"The contents of both saddlebags. Empty it all out onto the ground."

"B-But . . . my stuff'll get dirty."

"Your stuff can get dirty or you can get dead," Roper said. "Your choice."

Word had gotten around that something was happening on the street, so it was clear, but faces were pressed up against windows, and that included the saloon.

"A-All right, wait," Stark said. He went to his horse, removed both saddlebags, and started to put his hand in one.

"How stupid do you think I am? You go for a gun in there and I'll shoot you in the face."

It had been Roper's experience that nobody wanted to get shot, but the prospect of getting shot in the face seemed to be worst of all.

Stark pulled his hand out of his saddle-bags. He took them off his horse and dumped the contents on the ground.

"Back up," Roper said.

Stark obeyed. Roper kicked the contents around on the ground, saw a dirty shirt, a coffee cup, a pot, some letters, some loose bullets, and the extra gun Stark had been reaching for.

"If you had pulled that gun, I would have killed you, son," Roper said.

"Yessir."

"Now I'm going to ask you for the last time," Roper said. "Did anyone hire you to brace me?"

"No, sir, we wuz just gonna rob you."

"Rob me and kill me, is more likely. I'm leaving town, so you better get out of my sight before I change my mind."

"My things," Stark said, "my horse, and guns —"

"You come back for them later, if they're still here," Roper said. "Right now, just get the hell out of my sight."

Stark hesitated, then turned and ran off down the street.

Roper holstered his gun, left Stark's belongings on the ground, where anybody could go through them. He took a quick look at the letters, but they weren't anything of concern to him.

He picked up the extra gun and stuck it in his belt and went back into the saloon and up to the bar.

"Still say you don't know those boys?" he asked the bartender.

"That's a fact, mister. Why'd you let them go?"

"I don't have time to have them arrested and go to court. I've got to get moving." Plus, he'd already killed three men this trip who had intended to rob him. He wasn't looking to repeat the experience.

"Well, have another beer, on the house."

"Don't mind if I do."

Roper nursed his beer and talked to the bartender about who the law was in Sedona.

"Name's Hardesty, Al Hardesty. Been sheriff here for a few months."

"First-time lawman?"

"Naw, he's wore a badge in other towns. Must be about forty, ol' Al. It's only this job that's new to him."

"You know a fella in Jerome named Henry Wilkins?" Roper asked.

"Sure, I know ol' Henry. Stops in here when he comes to town for supplies."

"You know when he was here last?"

The man rubbed his jaw and said, "Must

be a few weeks now. He usually comes in once a month. He's got him a small ranch, raises some horses."

"Is there a telegraph office in town?"

"Yeah, but if you're thinkin' of sendin' one to Jerome, forget it. They ain't got one."

Roper wasn't thinking about sending one to Jerome. He was thinking of sending two to Denver.

"Okay," he said, "thanks for the beer, and the information."

"Come back if you're stayin' in town."

"I'm not staying, but I may be back. How about directing me to the telegraph office?"

He left the saloon and started toward the telegraph office, following the bartender's directions.

Roper had some men in Denver he used when he needed extra help. He was going to send telegrams to two of them, get them moving on a new plan he had, and then head for Jerome.

If someone was using him to find these men so they could be killed, or if they were ahead of him, he was going to take steps to protect the remaining three.

Telegraph office first.

37

Having sent his telegrams to Denver, hoping there'd be a reply by the time he got back to Sedona, Roper mounted up and rode to Jerome to find Henry Wilkins.

Jerome was about twenty miles from Sedona. Roper rode the horse hard and made the ride in two-and-a-half hours. There wasn't much to Jerome, which had fallen on hard times. Many of the buildings were boarded up, but there was a saloon, a hotel, a livery, and the sheriff's office. However, the bartender in Sedona had already told Roper that Wilkins had a ranch on the outside of town, so he rode through Jerome without stopping.

Hoping he wouldn't arrive to find Wilkins dead, Roper rode up to the ranch, which consisted of a house, a barn, and a corral. There were a few horses in the corral, but nothing to indicate that anyone was raising them for sale.

He rode up to the house and dismounted.

"Wilkins," he shouted. "Henry Wilkins!"

He looked around, anxiously waiting for someone to appear from the house or the barn. Whoever had killed Quinn had only just beaten him to the man, so he drew his gun, just in case.

"Stand fast, friend," he heard a voice say from behind him. Roper put his hands up.

"What are you doin' here?"

"I'm looking for Henry Wilkins," Roper said, hoping he wasn't talking to the man who had killed Quinn, and maybe Wilkins as well.

"That's me. Who are you?"

"My name's Roper," Roper said. "I'm a private detective from Denver. Are you Wilkins?"

"I am."

"Can I put my hands down?"

"I got a rifle pointed at you," Wilkins said. "Holster your weapon and turn around slowly."

Roper obeyed, sliding the pistol into the holster and turning. He continued to hold his hands away from his body so as to appear less threatening.

"What are you doin' here?" Wilkins asked. He was a tall man with very long, stringy hair, painfully thin, as if he hadn't been eating well for a long time. "Why are you look-ing for me?"

"Well," Roper said, "basically I'm here to save your life."

"What?"

"If we could go inside and talk, I can explain."

"First tell me who sent you."

"Victoria Westover." Roper decided it didn't matter whether they went inside, or stayed out.

"Westover?" Wilkins said. The barrel of the rifle lowered slightly. "I knew a Westover during the war. Howard Westover?"

"That's right," Roper said. "Victoria is his wife. She sent me to find you."

"Why?"

"He's in a bad way," Roper said, "and he's in danger of having his Medal of Honor stripped from him."

"Stripped?"

"That's right. She sent me to find five men he served with so they can swear he earned the medal honorably."

"And I'm one of the five?" Wilkins seemed surprised.

"Do you remember Vincent McCord and Gerald Quinn?" Roper asked.

"I do," Wilkins said, and the barrel dipped even more, until it was pointing at the ground. "I served with them."

"They're dead."

"What? How?"

"McCord died years ago, in Saint Joe, Missouri," Roper said, "but someone killed Quinn days ago, before I could get to him. And I think that same someone is after you."

"Me? Somebody wants to kill me?"

"Yes," Roper said, "and they may not be far behind me. They beat me to Quinn, but it looks like I beat them to you. We have to get out of here."

"And go where?"

"Somewhere I can keep you safe," Roper said.

"I can take care of myself."

"You're an old soldier, I know," Roper said. "So am I. I served with Pinkerton."

"They didn't call him that during the war," Wilkins said.

"I know, he was Major E. J. Allan. I'm a private detective now because of him."

Wilkins looked around, then said, "You better come inside."

"Only long enough for you to pack," Roper said. "We've got to get out of here."

"Come inside," Wilkins said. "We can talk more over a jug."

The hard ride had awakened a thirst in

Roper so he said, "All right. One drink and then we're out of here!"

38

The house was little more than a bare cabin inside, but there was a rickety table and two matching chairs. It reminded him of the house Vincent McCord's woman lived in.

"Have yourself a seat," Wilkins said. "I'll get the jug," Roper was feeling antsy. Could be a killer outside any minute. He had to get Wilkins out of there. Anyplace other than this would do.

Wilkins returned with a jug, sat across from Roper, and passed it to him. The detective uncorked it and poured some down his throat. It burned like fire. He put it on the table and pushed it back, his eyes tearing.

Wilkins drank deeply from the jug, then put the cork back in. He must have been in his thirties during the war, because he looked to be near sixty.

"You better start from the beginning, mister."

"I don't think we have time, Mr. Wilkins. I'm convinced there's a man on the way here to kill you. If we don't get you out of here —"

"You sure about this?"

"Sure as I can be," Roper said. "Gerald Quinn is dead, and there are two more men on my list."

"Who are they?"

"David Hampstead and Zack Templeton." Wilkins sat back in his chair.

"You know them?" Roper asked.

"I served with both of them."

"I guess that's why she gave me your names, then. You got a horse?"

"A broke-down saddle mount one in the back."

"Why don't you pack what you've got, saddle that horse, and we'll get out of here."

"And go where?"

"Anywhere, just so long as I keep you alive."

"You're serious about this."

"Yes, I am. After this I'm going to see Hampstead and Templeton."

"I ain't seen them boys in years," Wilkins said. "Okay, I'll do it. I ain't got much, it'll all fit in some saddlebags."

"Get them packed, then," Roper said. "I'll watch your back while you saddle up."

"That stuff you said about Westover true? They want his medal?"

"They're recalling many medals," Roper said. "His is one of them."

"For sure?"

"No, not for sure," Roper said. "Pack up and I'll tell you about it while you saddle up."

"Okay."

Behind the house, Wilkins saddled his horse, which would probably barely carry him to Sedona. When they got there, they'd have to get him a better mount. The rest of the horses he released, so they wouldn't starve to death.

"Where we goin'?" Wilkins asked.

"We'll start with Sedona," Roper said. "I'm expecting a couple of telegrams."

Roper made sure Wilkins didn't get shot while he saddled his horse, and then they both mounted up. The only gun Wilkins had was his rifle.

"You want a handgun? I've got an extra."

"I see that, sewed onto your saddle. That's pretty handy. But no, I ain't much use with a handgun. My rifle will do."

"All right, then," Roper said. "We better get moving. After I get my telegrams, I'm going to want to ride fast."

"What about me?"

"I got a piece of paper I want to show you," Roper said, "but that'll hold until we get to Sedona."

They rode to the front of the house. Wilkins reined in and looked around.

"Sorry you've got to leave your place," Roper said. "But you can come back in the future."

"Don't worry about that," Wilkins said. "It was never much of a ranch anyway."

"Then we'd better get moving."

Roper kept alert as they rode away from the ranch, on the watch for a bushwhacker or backshooter.

About a half an hour after they left, Kilkenny rode up to the Wilkins ranch. He dismounted, drew his gun, and entered the house. It was empty. He came out and looked around. There were horses in the corral, but no saddle in the barn. And on the ground he saw the tracks of two horses.

Talbot Roper had beat him here, and now he was on the run with Wilkins. But where would they go? Most likely Sedona, but at some point Roper was going to head for Hampstead and Templeton.

Unless Kilkenny beat him there.

39

When Roper and Wilkins rode into Sedona, they stopped at the telegraph office first. Roper made Wilkins come inside with him so he wouldn't catch a bullet.

"My telegrams come in?" he asked the clerk.

"Right soon after you left, mister," the man said. "Here ya go."

Roper accepted the telegrams and read them both, then smiled, folded them, and put them in his pocket.

"What do they say?"

"That some plans I've made are in motion," Roper said.

"Now all I need is for you to sign an affidavit and I'll be on my way."

"Nothin' doin'," Wilkins said.

"What?"

"I ain't signin' no paper until I see Hampstead and Templeton."

"You want to come with me?"

"You got the idea," Wilkins said.

"Well," Roper said, "that ought to keep you one step ahead of a bullet. Okay, let's get outfitted and get moving."

"In the dark?"

"We can't wait," Roper said. "There's a killer after you."

"Ain't he after you, too?"

Roper looked at him and said, "You'd think so, wouldn't you."

It puzzled Roper. If the killer was the one who had taken a shot at him in Washington, why hadn't he tried out on the trail? He was sure he'd been in the man's crosshairs at least once.

They outfitted themselves from the general store with just enough supplies for them each to carry some. Then they went to the livery, where Roper used a portion of his expense money to buy Wilkins a fresh horse.

"Ain't had an animal this sound under me in a while," he said as they moved his saddle onto it.

"What about the ones you had in your corral?"

"Second-rate," Wilkins said. "Ever since the war, I been nothin' but second-rate."

Roper didn't know what to say to that. He couldn't very well tell a man he just met that he was wrong.

They walked their horses outside, Roper checking the corners and rooftops.

"You really are worried about a shooter, aren't you?" Wilkins said.

"I am."

They mounted up and rode out.

Kilkenny was angry.

He rode into Sedona behind the tracks left by Roper and Wilkins, but he knew he wasn't going to be able to follow them out. Not tonight. He wouldn't be able to track them in the dark.

He put his horse up at the livery, got himself a room at the smallest, cheapest hotel in town. Then he had a hot meal, wondering why he'd taken this job in the first place. It was a lot of time on the trail for not much of a payoff. He knew the payoff would come in the end, but getting to the end was taking longer than he liked.

There was no doubt in his mind that Roper was going to head north — but to where? The logical place would be Montana, and David Hampstead. He was next in line — but what if Roper didn't stick to the list?

He wondered if Roper had sent any telegrams while he was in town. That was something he would be able to check in the morning, when the office opened. Might even send a telegram of his own. At the moment there was nothing he could do but have a few beers and then turn in. Get started back on the job in the morning. Because that was all it was to him, a job.

Like any other job.

Roper and Wilkins got away from Sedona, headed north, and then camped.

"We could've spent a night in a hotel," Wilkins said, sitting across the fire from Roper.

"I wanted to get out of town," Roper said. "A killer could have tracked us that far. But he can't track us at night."

"Unless he's part Injun."

Wilkins made a good point. Roper wondered just what kind of killer was on his trail — or to be more precise, Wilkins's trail.

Half Indian.

That wouldn't be so good. Any man with Indian blood would be able to track them no matter what he did. Roper was a great detective, but to his mind just an adequate cowboy. Even if the shooter was a professional bounty hunter, his trail knowledge would be better than Roper's. The detective was a man who knew his limitations.

"Let's just figure he's not part Injun," Roper said, "and act accordingly."

40

Roper decided not to go north, but north-east. When they got to Albuquerque, they caught the train, took it toward Denver. He wasn't interested in going back to Denver, but since they had to change trains there, he decided to spend one night and catch a train in the morning. He also decided to turn Nickel over to Wilkins, and pick up his own horse.

He stashed Wilkins in a small hotel he used for hiding people. Then he went to his office. He unlocked the front door and entered, was glad to find the reception desk empty. He figured Mrs. Batchelder kept sending Lola over, but apparently today wasn't one of those days. He went into his office and sat behind his desk. He ran his hand over his face, felt the two-day stubble there. He also felt fatigue in his bones. Later he'd go home, have a hot bath and a shave, and be ready to kick off again the next day.

He looked on his desk and found two messages, one each from the men he'd sent telegrams to.

First Sally Bando. His real name was Salvatore Bandini. He'd come to the United States twenty years earlier from Italy, made his way to Denver, working mostly as a strike breaker for disreputable private detective agencies. There he met Roper, who put him to work from time to time on more honest matters.

Sally left a message that said he was on his way to Montana as Roper had instructed. He left the message just in case Roper stopped in there. He also said if he had anything to report, he'd send a telegram to Mrs. Batchelder. Roper also paid her to be a go-between when he was on the trail.

The other message was left by Tommy Dexter, who did the same kind of work for him as Sally Bando. His message said he was on his way to South Dakota, and that Roper was going to owe him if he lost any toes to frostbite. He made the same comment about sending further messages to Mrs. Batchelder.

He put the notes back on the desk, rubbed both hands over his face. Being in Denver wasn't smart. If the killer knew anything about him, he knew he was from Denver.

He might have come here to wait for him. The good thing was Roper knew every inch of Denver, and had contacts and, at least, a few friends.

He decided to go on home and have that bath and get started early the next morning.

The next morning, before picking up Wilkins, Roper stopped in at Mrs. Batch-elder's.

"Well, hello, handsome," she said from behind her desk. "Didn't know you were back."

"Back and gone again, Lily," he said. She was a handsome woman in her late forties. She had set up her business ten years earlier, and Roper still didn't know what she was doing before that.

"Are you checking for messages, telegrams?"

"I am."

"Well, nothing's come in yet," she said. "Where are you off to this time?"

"Can't say," he said, "but I'll send you a telegram from time to time. I'll wait an hour for an answer, and then move on."

"Are you in trouble, Tal?" she asked.

"Might be," he said. "But don't worry about it. I'll take care of it."

"If you say so," she said.

"I'm going to go out the back way, Lily," he said. "I'll lock it behind me."

As he left her office, she remembered the last time he'd gone out the back door. He'd been in real trouble that time. But he'd gotten out of it. She was sure he'd get out of it now.

Roper went to the hotel and picked up Wilkins.

"Sure did sleep good last night," Wilkins said as they left. "Can't remember the last time I slept so good. Real nice bed."

"It's not even one of the best hotels in town, Wilkins," Roper said. "I'm glad you liked it."

"Better than any hotel I ever stayed in before," Wilkins said. "It was fine, Roper, just fine."

"Come on," Roper said. "We've got to catch a train."

They picked up their horses — Nickel, and Roper's palomino — took them to the station, and put them on the stock car. Then they got on the train and took their seats.

"Where are we headed now?" Wilkins asked.

"We're going someplace nobody will

expect us to go," Roper sad. "At least, so I hope."

41

Edward Harwick looked up as Victoria Westover entered his office. He was surprised to see her. She came to town very infrequently. She was dressed for business, in a severe suit and hat.

"Victoria," he said, standing.

"Sit down, Edward," she said. "I just came to talk to you. I haven't heard from you in some time about Mr. Roper's progress."

Harwick sat back down, and Victoria sat across from him.

"I'm afraid that's because I haven't heard from him in a while," the lawyer said.

"What's going on?" she asked. "What's he doing, staying out of contact this long?"

"I don't know, Victoria."

"Do you think he's . . ."

"What? Dead?" he asked. "He's a man who can take care of himself."

"Maybe . . ." she said, and then stopped.

"Maybe what?"

"Maybe we should have told him the truth from the beginning."

Harwick stood up, walked around the desk, and put his hand on her shoulder.

"It's too late for that now, Victoria," he said. "Come on, I'll see you home. We'll hear from Roper soon. I'm sure of it."

He walked her out, wishing he were as confident as he sounded.

Donald White looked up as his office door opened. This was his real office, not the little empty room at Dupont Circle.

"Sir," Corporal Prince said. Prince's actual rank was lieutenant, but he was still undercover as a corporal. "You wanted to see me."

"Any word on Roper?"

"No, sir," Prince said. "He seems to have fallen off the face of the map."

"Not good, Prince," White said. "I wanted to keep an eye on him."

"Yessir."

"Well, all right, pack a bag."

"Sir?"

"You're going on a trip."

"Corporal Prince can't just leave, sir."

" 'Corporal Prince' just mustered out, soldier. You're back to being Lieutenant Prince."

"Yes, sir, thank you, sir," Prince said. "When am I leaving, sir?"

"Tomorrow morning."

"And where would I be going?"

White sat back in his chair and said, "I'll let you know tomorrow morning. Be back here at eight, I'll have a train ticket for you."

"Yes, sir," Prince said. "Would that be the time I'll also be learning what I'll be doing?"

"Yes, yes," White said, waving the man off, "you'll find out everything in the morning."

"Thank you, sir."

As the door closed behind the young lieutenant, Donald White wondered if he should have been more truthful with Talbot Roper. But he couldn't let friendship interfere with his job. He had known that years ago, when he first accepted this position. And nothing had changed since then. Nothing at all.

Tom Prince left the building with a feeling of excitement in his belly. He'd been undercover as "Corporal Prince" for some time. He was happy to be going back to Lieutenant Prince. He was also very pleased that it seemed he was being sent west to assist Talbot Roper.

Roper was a legend, not only as a detective, but from his experiences during the war, when he worked under Allan Pinkerton. Lieutenant Prince had heard all the stories about Roper and had been very excited to meet him. To be getting a chance to work with him was beyond a dream for him.

When Roper had been in Washington, Prince had not liked deceiving him. He'd be very happy to introduce himself properly and offer his help. Working with Talbot Roper would teach him a lot.

The soldier at the front door recognized Prince as a man of authority even without bars, and saluted him. Prince happily returned the salute. As "Corporal" Prince, he was the one always offering the salutes to others.

This was a nice change.

42

Roper and Wilkins rode into Gilette, Wyoming. The detective expected Sally Bando and Tommy Dexter to be there with their charges, David Hampstead and Zack Templeton. They did not have as far to come as he did, but he'd made parts of the trip by rail. He told Bando and Dexter to stay off trains and away from train stations. They were instructed to make the trip on horseback, stay away from towns, use pack mules so they didn't need to outfit more than once.

There were three hotels in Gilette, a medium-size town that was growing, just not as quickly as Cheyenne and Sheridan. He and Wilkins checked each hotel. The four men were not registered at any of them.

"Are there rooming houses in town?" Roper asked the clerk at the Gilette House (with three hotels in town, one of them had to have the word "House" in the name).

"Yes, sir," the clerk said. "We got two.

Both run by widows."

"Okay, we'll check them. Thanks."

The clerk told Roper where the rooming houses were, and he and Wilkins checked them, too.

The first was run by a woman named Mrs. Hawkins. She was in her sixties, told them she had four rooms to let and they were all full, but not with the men he was describing.

"I don't rent to anybody who looks like trouble," she added. "And I'm afraid that includes you two."

She closed the door in their faces.

The second rooming house was run by a younger woman. Mrs. Lawson was in her late forties, a widow who had turned her home into a rooming house in order to survive after her husband died.

"I ain't never gonna find another man like my Ralph," she told them, "so I got to do for myself."

She also said her rooms were full, but not with the men they were describing. She closed the door on them more gently, but Roper could see she had the same opinion of them that Mrs. Hawkins had.

"Come on," Roper said. "We'll register at one of the hotels."

"Which one?"

"Let's try the Gilette House."

They went back there and registered under assumed names. Roper got one room with two beds. He wanted to keep a close eye on Wilkins.

In the room, Wilkins sat on one of the beds.

"You don't think anyone was able to follow us here, do you?" he asked.

"Follow, no," Roper said. "Track, maybe."

"What do we do?"

"We wait."

"You said they'd be here waitin'."

"I said they should be here waiting," Roper said.

"So what do you think happened?"

"I don't know," Roper said. "Something must've held them up."

"But they're alive?"

"I sent good men to get them," Roper said. "They should be alive."

Wilkins thought a moment, then said, "Tell me again why we came to Gilette, Wyoming. I mean . . . what's here for us?"

"Nothing," Roper said, "and nobody. That's the point. Somebody is planning to kill the three of you. I don't know why. I decided to take all of you someplace neutral, and I picked Gilette because it's between

Helena, Montana, and Pierre, South Dakota."

"What are we gonna do when they get here?"

"We're going to talk," Roper said. "We're going to figure this out."

"What about those affidavits?"

"I don't know," Roper said. "I'll have to decide whether or not I'm still concerned with those."

"Ain't that the job you took on?" Wilkins asked. "To get them signed?"

"Somebody hasn't been truthful with me," Roper said. "I'm going to decide who that is."

"And then what?"

"And then I'm going to make them tell me the truth."

"And us?" Wilkins asked. "Me, Davey, and Zack?"

"I'm going to do my best to keep the three of you alive."

"I'm happy to hear that."

"When was the last time you saw any of these men?" Roper asked. "Any of the four of them?"

"The war," Wilkins said.

"Not since then?"

"No."

"No contact at all?"

"No."

"Why?" Roper asked. "Were there any hard feelings after the war?"

"No."

"What about between all of you and Westover?"

Wilkins hesitated, then said, "I think I'm gonna wait for the others to get here before I answer any more questions."

Well, Roper thought, that was part of an answer. There was definitely something going on that he didn't know about. He no longer felt any responsibility to keep in touch with the lawyer, Harwick, or Victoria Westover. They had both lied to him.

He still had to ascertain if Donald White had lied to him as well.

"How about some food?" Wilkins asked.

"I don't want you on the street," Roper said. "I'll go and get something and bring it up here."

"Okay," Wilkins said. He looked around. "I don't mind stayin' here. Nice room."

"Yeah," Roper said, walking to the door. "I'll be right back."

43

Roper found a small café and ordered a couple of steak dinners that he could take with him. As he headed back, he decided to stop in a saloon and get a bottle of whiskey they could share. He would have preferred beer, but he couldn't carry the food and two beers back to the room.

"I can give ya a bucket of beer, if ya want," the bartender told him. "And a coupla glasses ya could put in yer pocket."

"That sounds good," Roper said. "Let's do that."

While he waited, the smell of the steaks began to fill the room. There were two men sitting at a table together, close to the bar. Some others seated farther away didn't pay him any mind. These two, though, began to sniff the air.

"You got you a woman waitin' for you in your room?" one of them asked.

"No," Roper said. "Just me."

"Two steaks, two glasses, both for you?" the second man asked.

"I get hungry during the night," Roper said.

The two men exchanged a glance. They looked like a couple of ranch hands who had come into town for a beer or two. One of them got up and walked over alongside Roper, who didn't like it. He backed away a few steps.

"Hey, take it easy, friend," the man said.

"I don't like to be crowded," Roper said.

"Hey, we're just wonderin' if you got yourself a good-lookin' woman in your room," the man said. "This town ain't got much in the way of women."

"Even if I did, why would I tell you?"

"Well, we'd be willin' to chip in on whatever you're payin' her."

"I don't think so."

The man frowned, obviously taking offense. "Whatsa matter, you don't like to share?"

"No, I don't."

"Well, what about this?" The man lifted the napkin off one of the dinners. "How about sharing one of these steaks?"

"I thought we just established that I don't like to share."

Roper did not want to attract attention

while he was in Gilette, but this idiot would interpret that statement as cowardice.

The bartender came out with the pail of beer and two glasses. They weren't shot glasses, but they were small enough to fit in Roper's pockets — as long as he didn't have to bend over.

"Here ya go," the man said. "Leave the man alone, Hobie, he's a stranger in town."

"I know it," Hobie said, "but me and Jake was just tryin' to be friendly."

"Well, maybe he ain't lookin' for new friends."

"Why you takin' his side, Lou?" Hobie demanded.

"Because he's a customer of mine. If you're gonna start bothering my customers, I ain't gonna let you come in here."

"Now, see there?" Hobie asked, looking at Roper. "You done got me in trouble with Lou."

"You got yourself in trouble, friend," Roper said, collecting his things. He had the glasses perched in his pockets, the pail had a handle, and he'd have to balance the tray of steaks on one hand. As soon as he did that, though, he knew he'd be vulnerable.

"I'm going now," he said to the man. "Are we going to have any trouble?"

"Trouble?" Hobie asked. "We ain't lookin' for trouble, are we, Jake?"

"No trouble here," Jake said.

Hobie walked back to the table and sat down.

"Enjoy your steak," Hobie said, "and your woman."

Roper picked up his tray and left.

When he got to the hotel room, he kicked the door with the toe of his boot. Wilkins opened it and asked, "What took ya so long? I'm starved."

"I stopped to get some beer, and a couple of guys tried to make friends with me."

"Who were they?"

Roper walked in, kicked the door shut.

"I don't know," he said. "Locals. The bartender knew them."

"So we ain't gonna have no trouble from them?"

"I don't think so," Roper said. "Not the kind of trouble we're worried about anyway. They just thought I had a girl in my room. Apparently they don't have that many available women in town."

"That's too bad," Wilkins said. "You brung knives and forks?"

"I did," Roper said.

He doled out the silverware and they sat

246

on their bed to eat.

"I could use me a woman about now," Wilkins said.

"I think we're going to have to keep low profiles, Wilkins," he said. "No restaurants, no women. We just have to keep to ourselves until the others get here."

"What if they don't get here?"

"They will, don't worry," Roper said. "I can depend on my men."

"Ain't it nice to know that," Wilkins said.

"You served in the war with men you could depend on, didn't you?"

Wilkins hesitated, then said, "There was a time I thought so."

"So you couldn't depend on Hampstead and Templeton?" Roper asked.

Wilkins hesitated, frowned, then said, "I don't wanna talk about nothin' until I see them."

"That's up to you." Roper felt he could have pushed the matter, but decided against it. Maybe when the three survivors got together, he'd finally find out what was really going on.

They ate their meal and drank their beer, talking all the while. They had done a lot of talking during the trip, but somehow never seemed to have trouble finding a subject.

This time Wilkins kept asking questions about being a detective. Roper answered them as honestly as he could.

"I suppose," he said at one point, "if I hadn't met Pinkerton during the war and started working for him, I wouldn't be a detective right now."

"How old was you?"

"I was a youngster when I met him," Roper said. "He saw something in me, took me under his wing."

"Then how come you ain't a Pinkerton detective?" Wilkins asked. "Workin' for him?"

"I was a Pink for a while, but I decided to go out on my own."

"How did he take that?"

"Not well," Roper said. "He seemed to take that as a betrayal."

"You see him much?"

"No, he wasn't talking to me for a long time, and now he's dead, so . . ."

"Too bad."

They finished eating and Roper collected all the paraphernalia.

"I told the folks who gave me this stuff I'd bring it back as soon as we finished."

"Can't it wait 'til mornin'?" Wilkins asked.

"It'll only take me a few minutes."

"What if you run into yer new friends?"

Wilkins asked. "Who's gonna watch yer back?"

"The saloon's right across the street," Roper said. "You can see it from the window. I don't think anything'll happen."

He carried everything to the door, which Wilkins opened for him.

"Thanks. I'll be right back."

Roper left the room and Wilkins closed the door behind him. He went back to his bed and sat down, but made up his mind very quickly. He stood up, picked up his rifle, walked to the window, and opened it. He watched Roper walk down the street, but he was more interested in the saloon across the street. It was dark, but there was enough moonlight to illuminate the street.

He got down on his knees, leaned the rifle barrel in the windowsill, and settled down to watch.

44

Roper's first stop was the saloon to return the bucket. As he entered, he saw that very little had changed in the two hours he'd been gone. The same number of men were sitting at tables, and nobody was leaning on the bar. Hobie and Jake had not moved, but they sat up straight as he entered.

"Hey, back so soon?" Hobie asked. "Guess that gal you got ain't much, huh?"

"Hey, they probably just finished eatin', Hob," his friend said. "Now he's gonna go back and see how good she is."

"Here's your bucket," Roper said to the bartender, ignoring the two men. "Thanks a lot."

"Another while you're here?" the bartender asked.

He would have liked one, but that would have been tempting fate. He could feel that Hobie and Jake behind him were aching for trouble.

"Thanks for the offer. I've got to get back
—"

"Won't take the time for a free beer!" Hobie called out, standing up. "In a hurry to
get back to your room?"

"You got law here?" Roper asked the bartender.

"Yeah, we got a sheriff. Are we gonna need
him?"

"I don't know," Roper said. "Suppose you
tell me."

"Them two are troublemakers, all right,"
the bartender said.

"How far are they going to push it?"

"As far as you'll let them, I guess."

"Great. I'll have that beer. No, just give
me a beer mug."

"A mug?"

"Right."

"An empty mug?"

"Right."

"Okay."

The bartender put an empty mug on the
bar.

"I tol' you ya shoulda let us come to your
room and help you with that gal," Hobie
said. "Now yer insultin' us by not taking a
free beer with us. Whataya think of that,
Jake?"

"I think it's —" Jake started, but he

stopped short when Roper turned, took two steps, and hit Hobie on the head with the empty mug. The man went down like a sack of shit.

The mug didn't break, so Roper brandished it in Jake's face and asked, "What do you think of that, Jake?"

"Oh . . ." Jake said, staring at the detective with wide eyes.

"Tell your buddy when he wakes up that if he sees me again, he's to keep his mouth shut. Understand?"

"I — uh — I understand."

"Good." Roper took the mug and set it back on the bar, said to the bartender, "Thanks."

"Sure."

Roper walked out and headed for the café.

While Roper was returning the tray, plates, and utensils to the café, Jake poured some cold beer on Hobie's face to wake him up.

"What the hell happened?" Hobie demanded.

"That fella hit you with a mug," Jake said.

"What?" Hobie got to his feet, looked around. "Where'd he go?"

"Guess he went to the café to bring back their stuff," the bartender said.

"That sonofabitch!" Hobie said. "I'll kill him."

"Hobie, he says if you see him again, you better keep yer mouth shut," Jake said.

"I'll keep my mouth shut," Hobie said, "while I'm killin' him!"

"You're gonna need help," the bartender said. He took a pistol out from beneath the bar.

"You!" Hobie said. "You gave him the empty mug to hit me with."

"I didn't know what he was gonna do with it," the bartender said. "Hell, he was askin' about the sheriff."

"Well, goddamnit, let's go outside and get him, then," Hobie said. "Are ya with me?"

"I am," Jake said.

"Me, too," the bartender said. "Can't let a stranger get away with that."

"No, we sure as hell can't," Hobie said. He looked at the rest of the men in the saloon. "Anybody else comin' with us?"

Nobody moved.

"Fine!" Hobie said. "Don't nobody come outside until it's all over."

Roper was walking back from the café, and as he came within sight of the saloon, he thought he better cross the street. As he started to do that, the batwing doors opened and three men came out. He recognized them as Hobie, Jake, and the bartender. It looked like the bartender was taking their side.

"Hey, stranger!" Hobie shouted.

Roper stopped in the middle of the street and turned.

Wilkins watched from the window as three men came out of the saloon and braced Roper. He brought the rifle to his shoulder, sighted down the barrel, practically over Roper's shoulder. The detective was doing everything he could to keep him alive. It was time for Wilkins to return the favor.

"What do you fellas want now?" Roper asked.

"You can't get away with cold-cocking me with a beer mug," Hobie said.

"You wouldn't shut up any other way," Roper told him.

"You wanna shut me up, do it like a man, with your gun," Hobie said.

"You want to die that bad?"

"That's big talk from one man facing three," Hobie said.

"Two cowhands and a bartender," Roper said.

"You got a big mouth, you know, mister?"

the bartender said.

"Your friends are the ones who started this with their mouths," Roper said. "I'm willing to let it drop and go to my room. I'm tired."

" 'Fraid we can't do that, mister," Hobie said. "We can't let strangers come into our town and treat our folks this way."

"I didn't treat your folks in any way," Roper said. "I treated you that way. Why don't you tell your friends to go back into the saloon and you and me will settle this man-to-man."

"Hell," Hobie said, "he's scared!"

Roper wondered how, with all the towns he could have chosen, he'd actually picked Gilette, which seemed to be populated by morons. It never occurred to him that these were part of the whole Howard Westover affair. They were obviously just locals who liked to hoorah strangers.

Damn it, he was either going to end up dead or involved with the local law. And he didn't particularly look forward to either outcome.

45

Talbot Roper was not a gunfighter. He was not a fast gun. He was able to hit what he shot at, and he reacted during this kind of situation calmly. It was not the fastest gun who survived, but the most accurate. But facing these three men, he knew that one of them was bound to get a true shot off. They were not the Castle brothers in Los Lunas. These were men who were more used to using their guns.

This would be a lot more difficult.

Wilkins decided to key on the man in the center. Flanked as he was by the other two men, it pointed him out as the leader. The minute he touched his gun, Wilkins would kill him.

Hobie Patton fancied himself a fast gun. He was the fastest draw and the best shot on his ranch, and he'd won the turkey shoot every year for the past five years.

He was ready to put this stranger in the ground.

His friend, Jake Weaver, wished he were back in the saloon with a beer in his hand.

The bartender, Lou McCarver, had his gun tucked into his belt. He'd been in plenty of brawls in his saloon, and plenty of shootouts there, but he'd never been involved in a shootout on the street. He wanted to get this over with because he had a lot of dirty glasses behind the bar.

Roper kept his eyes on Hobie, standing in the center. Jake looked scared. And the bartender looked distracted. He had to take Hobie first. On the other hand, the light was on in his room and he saw Wilkins in the window. From up there, he figured Wilkins would pick Hobie out as his target. He was better off concentrating on the other two. He was going to be real angry if he got killed by a distracted bartender.

"Go ahead, Hobie," he called out. "It's your play to call."

"Don't rush me, friend," Hobie said. "Don't be in such a hurry to die —"

Hobie went for his gun, surprising even his two partners. He'd hoped that talking to Roper would distract him.

Roper heard the rifle shot from behind him, just a split second before he fired his own gun twice. The air filled with the sound and smell of gunfire and then suddenly it was quiet.

Roper saw that all three men were down. His gun was still in his hand. He looked down at himself, didn't see any blood. He used his left hand to check himself out, but there were no holes. Apparently, he had come out of the situation unscathed. He didn't know how many times Wilkins had fired from the window, but at least that first shot was true.

He walked to the three fallen men, noticing the men who were crowded around the batwing doors. Then he heard somebody yell, "Lou's dead! Free beer!" and they all vanished back inside.

Roper checked the three bodies, found them all dead. What now? Wait around for the law and an undertaker? Go back to his room and let them come to him?

He waited a few minutes but nobody came running. Shootings couldn't have been that common in Gilette. He looked around, shrugged, and went back into the hotel.

Wilkins backed out of the window after

Roper checked the three bodies and closed it behind him. As far as anyone down there knew, Roper had gunned down the three men. As far as Wilkins was concerned, he had partially paid his debt to Roper.

But there was another way to pay Roper back, and that was to sign an affidavit for him. Wilkins just didn't know if he could do that. At least, not until he talked with Hampstead and Templeton. It was too bad about McCord being killed all those years ago, but everyone who knew him knew that Vince McCord would end up that way, either in the war or after.

Gerald Quinn, that was a shame. Quinn was a good man, and Wilkins would have liked to help the detective find out who killed him.

But the rest . . . signing the affidavit, he couldn't make up his mind about that. At least, not until the other two arrived in Gilette.

If they got there at all.

46

Roper walked into the hotel, didn't see anyone at the clerk's desk. That was what bullets in the street usually did to people.

He went up the stairs, down the hall to his room, and entered.

Wilkins was sitting on the bed, his hands behind his head.

"Thanks."

"For what?" Wilkins asked.

"I don't know how many shots you fired, but that first one did the trick. I figured you'd target the center man first."

"I fired once," Wilkins said. "You were pretty good. I didn't have to pull the trigger again."

Roper nodded, ejected the spent shells from his gun, replaced them, and holstered it.

"We're liable to get a visit from the law tonight," he said. "I'll do the talking."

"Suits me," Wilkins said.

Roper walked to his bed and sat down.

"You didn't bring a bottle of whiskey, did you?" Wilkins asked.

"No," Roper said. "Just the beer."

"Too bad."

Roper agreed.

It only took half an hour for a knock to come at the door.

"Sooner than I thought," Roper said. "Remember, let me do the talking."

Wilkins nodded.

Roper went to the door and opened it, with his hand on his gun. Standing out in the hall was a tall man with a sheriff's badge. Behind him was a shorter, younger man, wearing a deputy's badge.

"You the fella from the street?" the sheriff asked. "Just shot three men?"

"I shot three men about half an hour ago," Roper said. "So I guess you want me, unless somebody else shot three men since then."

The sheriff looked at Roper's hand, which was on his gun.

"I'm gonna need you to identify yourself," the lawman said.

"You want me to do it here, or come to your office?" Roper asked.

"Here'll do," the sheriff said.

"Why don't you and your deputy come in, Sheriff . . . what's your name?"

"Freese," the lawman said, "Sheriff Freese."

"Come on in, Sheriff Freese."

The two lawmen entered, nodded to Wilkins, who was still sitting on his bed. His rifle was leaning against the wall next to him.

"This fella is Henry Wilkins," Roper said. "My name is Talbot Roper. I'm a private detective."

"Detective, huh?" Freese asked. "What brings you here, to Gilette?"

"I'm meeting some friends."

"Why here?"

Roper shrugged. "We had to meet somewhere. This is as good a place as any."

"You got something that says you're who you say you are?"

Roper went to his saddlebags, took out his wallet, and handed it to the sheriff. There were several pieces of identification there with his name and address on them.

"Denver, huh?"

"That's right."

Freese handed the wallet back.

"You wanna tell me what happened in the street, why you had to kill three of our citizens?"

"They pushed it, Sheriff," Roper said. "I gave them all the chance to walk away."

"I understand you had a run-in with Jake and Hobie in the saloon."

"With them, yeah," Roper said. "I don't know why the bartender was in the street. I had no beef with him, and as far as I knew, he had none with me."

"I got the story from the saloon," Freese said.

"And?"

"It's like you say," the lawman said. "Hobie was hoorahing you until you hit him with a beer mug."

"I put him down without killing him," Roper said. "He should have stayed down."

"I guess he should've," Freese said.

"If you want me to come to your office with you, Sheriff, I will," Roper said.

"There's no need," Freese said. "Your story checks out. They braced you in the street, and they called the play. I don't think I have any grounds to take you in."

"I appreciate that."

"But I do have the right to tell you to leave town."

"What?"

"Those boys all have friends in town," Freese said. "To keep any more trouble from happening, you have to leave."

"I told you, I'm waiting for some friends to get here," Roper said.

"I know that, but I can't have any more gunplay in the street. Your friend can wait here for the others, but you have to leave."

"No," Roper said, "I can't do that."

"If you don't leave," the sheriff said, "I'll have to put you in a cell."

"Are you serious?"

"I'm afraid I am."

The deputy drew himself up and stared at Roper. "You better do what the sheriff says."

Roper looked at the deputy, staring at him until the younger man averted his eyes.

"Okay, Sheriff," he said finally. "I'll be leaving first thing in the morning."

"Fine," Freese said. "Sorry about this, Mr. Roper, but there's nothing I can do."

Roper opened the door and waited while the sheriff and his deputy left.

"What are we gonna do?" Wilkins asked. "Should I stay and wait while you go?"

"No, I can't leave you here alone," Roper said. "We'll have to leave and camp just outside of town, try and catch the others when they ride in."

"Well," Wilkins said, "at least I get to sleep in a real bed one more night."

"Yeah," Roper said, "I could use some sleep myself."

■ ■ ■ ■

They each washed up with the pitcher and basin on the dresser. Wilkins got between the sheets, but before he went to bed, Roper took the chair from the corner and jammed it underneath the doorknob.

"Just in case," he told Wilkins.

"What about the window?"

"They'd have to scale the building to get in that way, but I'll put the pitcher on the windowsill just in case. They'd have to knock it off to get in."

"Good enough," Wilkins said.

Roper turned down the lamp on the wall by the door and got into bed.

47

Sally Bando passed a cup of coffee over to Dave Hampstead, who was wincing as he sat on the ground.

"Damn," Hampstead said, "it's been a while since I've been in the saddle."

Bando had seen that the moment he met Dave Hampstead in Montana. The man was a businessman and had the belly to prove it.

"My ass is used to sittin' in a chair, not on a horse," he went on. "Was the day I didn't have this belly and sore ass, but that was years ago."

"Sorry, Mr. Hampstead," Bando said, "but my orders are to get you to Gilette, on horseback, and alive."

"Well," Hampstead said, "I can't rightly object to the alive part, can I?"

"No, sir." Bando passed Hampstead a plate of bacon and beans, and a fork.

"Eat up, friend," Bando said. "We'll be in Gilette tomorrow."

"And then I get to find out what this is all about?" Hampstead asked.

"Then we all do," Bando said. He only knew what he and Dexter were hired to do, didn't know anything about a Medal of Honor, or about the first two dead men. His telegram from Roper simply said "Do this" and he was doing it.

In another camp, Tommy Dexter handed his charge, Zack Templeton, a plate of beans and a cup of coffee.

"We'll need to split the watch tonight again," he said.

"What for?" Templeton asked. "Who's chasing us?"

"I don't know if anyone is chasing us," Dexter said, "but I like to be careful."

Templeton must have been young during the war, because he barely looked forty now. When Dexter found him, he was working as a hand on a ranch. He spent his days in the saddle, so riding to Gilette, Wyoming, was no chore for him.

"I'll take the first watch, then," Templeton said. "You get some shut-eye."

"I can use it," Dexter said.

"Still not gonna tell me what this is all about?" Templeton asked.

"I told you all I know," Dexter said. "My

boss, Roper, he'll tell you the rest. And me, I hope."

"Well, I don't mind this," Templeton said. "It's better than punchin' cows, and I ain't seen those boys in a while. Not since the war."

"None of them since the war?"

"Nope. I heard about McCord dyin', but that wasn't no surprise. That boy was askin' for it."

Dexter didn't know what he was talking about. He knew nothing about McCord or Quinn. He only knew that Sally had been sent to pick up a man named Hampstead, and he had been sent to pick up Templeton. They were supposed to keep them alive and bring them to Gilette, Wyoming.

48

In the morning, Roper and Wilkins checked out of the hotel and chanced having breakfast before they left town. Roper took them to the café where he'd gotten the steaks the night before.

The sheriff came in while they were eating. His deputy stayed outside but cast mean looks toward them through the window.

"You gents mind if I have some coffee?" the sheriff asked.

"Be my guest, Sheriff," Roper said. The man sat. "Thanks for leaving your deputy outside. He's got a bad attitude."

"Yeah, he does," Freese said, "but he'll get over it. He just needs to live long enough to get a little older."

Freese poured himself some coffee, and a waiter brought a fresh pot over for them.

"Thanks, Lance," Freese said.

"Sure, Sheriff."

"We're ready to go, Sheriff," Roper assured him. "Just wanted to get some hot food in our bellies."

"Where you headed when you leave here?" Freese asked. "Maybe I can tell your friends when they get here."

"Don't worry 'bout it, Sheriff," Roper said. "We're going to try to catch them on the trail."

"I checked you out, Roper."

That didn't surprise Roper. He'd seen the telegraph wires as they rode into town. He didn't want to send any telegrams from here, though, just in case somebody was in Denver, waiting.

"You got a solid reputation."

"I like to think so."

"Can't imagine what brought you to Gilette, though."

"Afraid I can't say," Roper said.

"Well," Freese said, "that's up to you. Sorry I can't change my mind on you leavin'."

"Forget it," Roper said. "You've got your town to think of."

"Appreciate you takin' it that way."

The sheriff pushed back his chair and stood up. He hadn't taken a sip of his coffee.

"Good luck to you," he said and left.

"What was that about?" Wilkins asked.

"He checked me out, wants us to know he's not a bad guy."

"What do we do about meeting the others?" Wilkins asked. "From what you told me, they're coming from two different directions."

"We'll have to find a high point from where we can watch the town," Roper said. "High enough to be able to see both ends. It's not a big place."

"Think that's gonna work?"

"We won't know until we try."

Kilkenny tracked Roper to Denver. From there he sent out a batch of telegrams of his own and recruited some men right there in the city. He also got word from his men in Helena and Pierre that both Hampstead and Templeton were gone. That meant Roper was moving them, probably to some central location.

When he found Roper and his people, he was going to have a gang of his own to throw at them. Until then, he was content to remain in Denver until he got some word. Talbot Roper would be somewhere north of there, since Hampstead was in Montana and Templeton was in South Dakota. Denver was a good place to wait because wherever they had to go, they'd be able to get there pretty quick.

Kilkenny was sitting in a saloon on Market Street when one of his men, Chris Dunn, came in.

"What the hell are you doin' here, Dunn? You're supposed to be sittin' on the telegraph office," Kilkenny said.

"I was," Dunn said, taking a seat, "but I thought you might like to hear a piece of news that came in."

"News?"

Dunn nodded.

"There was a fella there from the *Post*," the man explained, "got hisself a piece of news he's gonna put in the paper this afternoon, but you're gettin' it before anybody else."

"What is it?"

"There was a shootout in Gilette, Wyoming," Dunn said. "One fella, from Denver, gunned down three men in the street."

"And why would that interest me, Dunn?" Kilkenny asked.

"Fella's name was Talbot Roper."

Kilkenny grinned.

"Yeah," Dunn said, "I figured —"

"Get the men together," Kilkenny told him. "Meet me at the railroad station in two hours."

"Horses?"

"Horses, guns, the works," Kilkenny said. "We got him."

49

It took half the day to circle the town and find a clearing where they could camp and look down at the town.

"This would be a great place to build a house," Wilkins said as they made camp.

"Well, keep it in mind," Roper said.

"I don't got any money to build a house," Wilkins said. "I'll probably have to go back to my place when this is over — if I'm still alive."

"You'll be alive," Roper said. "I'm not spending all this time with you to let you get killed."

"I appreciate that," Wilkins said.

They got a fire going, a pot of coffee, and then drank it, looking down on Gilette, where lights were just starting to come on.

"Looks right pretty," Wilkins said.

"And peaceful," Roper said.

"Now that we're gone."

"Yes."

While Roper continued to stare down at the town, Wilkins dropped some bacon into a pan. Then he handed Roper a plateful, saying, "There's nothin' else to do while we watch."

Roper accepted the bacon and ate it with his fingers. Then Wilkins broke out the one bottle of whiskey they had bought before leaving Gilette.

"Take it easy on that," Roper said.

"I ain't gonna get drunk."

"That's not what I meant," Roper said. "We're going to need that to wash down our supper."

"Okay." Wilkins took another drink, then put the cork back in and set the bottle aside.

They had talked about a lot of things during the many days they'd been together now, but neither of them had really talked about Howard Westover.

"Tell me how Westover's doin'," Wilkins said.

"Not so good. He has a nurse twenty-four hours a day."

"What's wrong with him?"

Roper hesitated, then said, "I really don't know. All I was told is that he was wounded during the war, and when he came home, he kept getting worse."

Wilkins nodded.

"What do you know about it?"

"About what?" Wilkins asked. "I only know what you told me."

"I mean, about his wound," Roper said. "Do you know anything about him being wounded in battle?"

"No," Wilkins said, "I don't know anything. He wasn't wounded while we were together."

"Then when could it have happened?"

"I don't know," Wilkins said. "We mustered out and split up. It could have happened then."

"After Lee surrendered?" Roper asked. "That would have been ironic." But of all people, Roper knew that the war had not just stopped after Lee surrendered. There were Confederate soldiers who didn't buy into Lee's decision, who went on raiding and fighting. But that didn't negate the irony of the situation. Some men did die after the war was actually over.

"I'm getting sleepy," Wilkins said then.

"Get some shut-eye," Roper said. "All we're going to be doing is watching. It's going to be tiring. We'll do it in shifts."

Wilkins nodded, lay down with his head on his saddle, and pulled his hat down over his eyes.

Roper finished the rest of the bacon, took

a swig from the whiskey bottle, and settled in to watch . . .

Later Wilkins asked, "How are you gonna recognize them from here? It could be anyone ridin' into town."

"I'll recognize them," Roper said. "Sally rides a sorrel, Dexter a buckskin."

"And you got a palomino," Wilkins said. "Seems like detectives ride pretty flashy horses."

"We each got our own tastes," Roper said.

"You got a taste for palominos?"

"I've got a taste for good solid horses," Roper said. "At the time I was buying, he was the best I could find."

"Best money could buy?" Wilkins asked. "I ain't never had the money to buy a fine horse."

"It wasn't about money," Roper said. "It was about the best horse."

"You get some rest," Wilkins told him. "I'll watch awhile."

"Okay."

"A sorrel and a buckskin, huh?"

"That's right."

Wilkins nodded, took up position at the fire. He looked at the whiskey bottle but didn't touch it.

50

"How much further?" Dave Hampstead asked.

"Just up ahead," Sally Bando said. "A few miles."

"What are we gonna do if we get there and your friends aren't there?" Hampstead asked.

"We'll wait," Bando said, "that's what we'll do."

Hampstead looked around him, then down at himself.

"Look at me," he said. "I'm a mess, riding a horse for the first time in years, and just on your say-so — the say-so of a man I never met before."

"Hey," Bando said, "I had those other names, didn't I?"

"Yah, you did, but you didn't let me send a telegram or anything, to check it out."

Bando looked at him.

"You wanna go back?" he asked. "Strike

out by yourself? Is that what you wanna do?"

"By myself?" Hampstead said. "Not now, not here. No, I'm stuck now, aren't I?"

"Yah," Bando said, "we're all stuck, until Roper tells us what the hell is goin' on."

East of Gilette, Dexter and Zack Templeton were riding in silence. Templeton rode real easy, sat a horse like he was born to it. Dexter did most of his work in Denver, not out on a horse. He knew his colleague Bando rode all the time, but his own ass was sore from too many days in the saddle after too many days in the city. When he saw Bando, he knew the man would be very happy after several days on a horse.

"You okay?" Templeton asked.

"I prefer to travel by rail these days," Dexter said.

"Not me. I love bein' on a horse."

"We should be there pretty soon," Dexter said. "Maybe after Roper tells us what this is all about, I can take a train home."

Templeton looked behind them.

"What's wrong?"

"Nothin'."

"If you know something, or feel something, let me know now."

"I just been havin' this feelin' that somebody's followin' us."

"How long?"

"Last day or so."

Dexter reined in and looked back.

"How many?" he asked.

"Don't know," Templeton said. "Like I said, just a feeling."

"Well," Dexter said, "let's pick it up, then. I'd like to get there before nightfall."

Templeton nodded his agreement.

51

"Gonna be dark soon," Wilkins said around a mouthful of bacon and beans.

"Yeah," Roper said.

"We won't be able to see 'em if they ride in at night."

"Should be a full moon, like last night," Roper said.

"When was they supposed to be here?" Wilkins asked.

"Whenever they get here," Roper said. "It depended on what they found when they got to Templeton and Hampstead, and when they got started from Helena and Pierre."

Even through it was fall, this far north there was already a chill in the air. They huddled near the fire, their coats pulled tightly around them.

"Pierre," Wilkins said. "I don't even know where that is."

"South Dakota."

"Never been up that way. Have you?"

"Yep."

"You been all over, ain't ya?"

"Pretty much."

"You been to other countries?"

"Some."

"I ain't never traveled no place," Wilkins said. "Just been on my place since the war."

They stared down at the town for a few moments, and then Roper said, "Henry."

"Yeah?"

"Tell me what happened."

"Whataya mean, what happened? Where?"

"In the war."

Wilkins stared at him and said, "I still don't know what you mean —"

"Come on," Roper said. "When I told you I had some affidavits for you and the others to sign, I saw your face. Why don't you want to sign one?"

"I didn't say I didn't wanna sign one," Wilkins said. "I said I wanted to wait until I talked to Davey and Zack."

"Yes, but why? Is there some secret you've all got? Is that what nobody's telling me?"

"You got a client, Roper. Maybe she shoulda told you everythin' she was supposed to."

"And what didn't she tell me?"

"Ain't for me to say," Wilkins said.

"So when Hampstead and Templeton get here, if they say it's okay to talk, you'll all talk?"

"I ain't sayin' there's anythin' to talk about," Wilkins said, "but let's wait until they get here afore we talk any more about it, okay?"

"Sure," Roper said, "that's okay."

"What's that?"

"What?"

"Down there." Wilkins pointed. "I thought I saw something to the east."

Roper fished in his saddlebag and came out with a spyglass. He put it to one eye and extended it.

"How long you had that?" Wilkins asked.

"Since the war."

"Why didn't you take it out before now?"

"I haven't needed it before now."

He trained the spyglass east, peered through it, and saw two men on horseback — one of the horses a buckskin.

"You got good eyes, Henry," he said. "That's my man Dexter with Zack Templeton."

"Lemme see."

Roper handed over the spyglass. Wilkins put it to his eye and said, "That's Zack, all right. From here he ain't changed much."

"You can tell?"

Wilkins lowered the glass and looked at Roper.

"He still sits a horse like he was born to it."

Roper said, "You stay here."

"Where you goin'?"

"Down to get them and bring them here."

"Why don't I come with you?"

"Because I don't want to be noticed," Roper said. "One of us is enough to get them."

"You're gonna leave me up here alone?"

"Nobody knows where we are, Henry."

"Then why you worried about bein' noticed?"

Roper started saddling his horse and said, "Just wait here. I won't be long."

Wilkins continued looking through the spyglass while Roper finished saddling his palomino.

"Why don't you give that poor horse a name?" Wilkins asked.

"A smart man once told me it made no sense to name something you might someday have to eat."

He swung into the saddle as Wilkins said, "Jesus, I'd never eat a horse."

"You ever been hungry enough to eat a horse?" Roper asked.

"Well, yeah, but —"

"Don't knock it until you've tried it."

52

Actually, Roper had not given the palomino a name because he couldn't think of a good one. So he ended up calling him "Boy" or "Big Boy" or "Big Fella" and they got along just fine.

He tried to figure a good point at which to intercept the two riders, and he hoped he'd be able to do it without getting shot.

"Stop!"

"What is it?" Templeton asked.

They reined their horses in.

"Listen," Dexter said.

They both listened for a few seconds, and then Templeton said, "That's a horse."

"And it's not comin' from behind us," Dexter pointed out.

"Okay," Templeton said, "so somebody's comin' toward us?"

"Sounds like it. Over here, quick."

Dexter led Templeton to a stand of rocks

large enough for them to hide behind.

"Let's see who it is," he said, drawing his gun. "If he's a stranger, we'll let him go by."

"Maybe he'll run into whoever's followin' us and they'll kill each other."

"That would be helpful," Dexter said, and then, "Shh," as the rider got closer.

Wilkins saw what Roper was doing, riding down to cut the two men off before they reached town. But he also saw the two men stop, and then hide behind some rocks. He tried to figure a way to signal Roper, thinking about a shot, but that would have just alerted everybody.

Helplessly, he watched and hoped the men wouldn't startle each other and start shooting.

Roper urged his horse on, hoping he hadn't missed the two riders. He looked up where Wilkins was. Too bad the man couldn't signal him.

He got down to where he thought a good intercept point would be, but they weren't there. He decided to just keep riding east.

"Hold it!" somebody shouted from just behind him.

"Dexter, you ass, you want to get yourself shot?" Roper shouted.

Dexter came out from behind a rock, leading his horse and laughing.

"How the hell are you, Roper?"

"Looking for you."

"You saw us comin'?" Dexter asked.

"Saw you? Hell, you make so much damn noise, I heard you. Where's Templeton?"

"Right here." A tall man in his forties came from behind the rocks, leading a horse of his own.

"Nice to see you safe and sound, Mr. Templeton. I got a friend of yours up there waiting to see you."

"Wilkins?"

"That's right. Why don't you two mount up?"

"We better," Dexter said. "We got somebody doggin' our trail."

"What?" Roper turned to look. "Where?"

"A ways back," Dexter said, mounting up. "Templeton felt him first, and then me."

"Wilkins is up high with a spyglass," Roper said. "Maybe he sees him. Let's go and find out."

When they rode into camp, Wilkins shouted immediately, "You got a tail!"

"You see him?" Roper asked.

"Yup."

"Show me."

"Hey, Henry," Templeton said.

"Zack, you ol' dog, you still sit a horse —"

"Let's put off the hellos until you show me," Roper said.

"Yeah, fine. Here." Wilkins handed him the spyglass. "A little east of town, just about where you picked these fellers up. He looks lost now."

Roper put the spyglass to his eye and looked down. Sure enough, he saw a man riding in small circles, like he wasn't sure where to go.

"How long's he been doggin' you, Tommy?" Roper asked Dexter.

"We only noticed him a day ago," Dexter said. "Could be longer."

Roper focused the spyglass, trying to get a closer look, because there was something familiar about the man. Only he wasn't sure . . .

"Shit," he said.

"What is it?" Dexter asked.

"I think I know this jasper."

"From where?" Wilkins asked.

"Whataya wanna do with him?" Tommy Dexter asked.

The man was close enough to take with a rifle shot, but that wasn't what Roper had in mind.

"The way he looks and the way he sits a horse . . ."

"Lemme see," Dexter said.

Roper handed the spyglass over.

"I see it," Dexter said. "He sits his horse like an Army man."

"Yeah, he does."

"Hell," Templeton said, "I still do that. Don't mean nothin'."

"But it's more than that," Roper said. "Tommy, cover him with your rifle. I'm going to go down and get him."

"When do you want me to kill him?" Dexter asked.

Roper mounted his horse, hesitated, then said, "As soon as you see that he brought somebody with him."

He rode out of camp again.

53

Roper rode harder than he had before. He wanted to get to the man before he started for Gilette. If he'd been tracking Templeton and Dexter since South Dakota, and lost them now, that would be unusual. However, if he was just following them, then he was confused by the fact that they were suddenly gone.

As he approached the point where he'd found Dexter and Templeton, he slowed his horse to a walk. When he didn't see the rider, he reined his horse in.

"Come on out!" he called.

He waited.

"Come on, I saw you from above. I know you're here."

Finally, the man rode his horse out from behind the same rock Dexter had used.

"Well," Roper said, "I thought I recognized you through my spyglass. Prince, right? I'm sorry, I don't remember your

291

rank. Private? Corporal?"

"Actually, it's lieutenant," Prince said.

"And what are you doing here, Lieutenant?" Roper asked.

"My boss sent me to find you," Prince said. "Or should I say, to help you."

"Really? And who would your boss be? No, wait, let me guess, my old friend Donny White."

"Mr. White is my boss, yes."

"You sit your horse too much like a soldier, Lieutenant," Roper said. "It's a dead giveaway."

"I'll have to remember that, Mr. Roper."

"Well, come on," Roper said. "We've got a fire and some coffee going."

"Lead the way, sir."

Roper led Prince to the camp, where they dismounted. All the other men eyed the young soldier with suspicion, until Roper introduced him.

"The lieutenant and I worked together in Washington," he said without getting more specific. "He was sent to help us apparently."

"How did he find us?" Wilkins asked.

"I went to Pierre to locate Mr. Templeton," Prince said. "I got there soon after he and Mr. Dexter had pulled out. I tracked them for a day, then caught sight of them. I've been following them since, figuring they would take me to Mr. Roper."

Wilkins looked at Roper.

"If he could do that, then anybody else could, too."

"There was no one else following," Prince said. "I'm quite sure of that."

"Somebody could've come up with the same plan," Dexter pointed out, "only they could've gone to Helena and started there."

"That's true," Roper said. "I was expecting Sally to get here today as well. If he and Dave Hampstead do get here, it'll be after dark."

"Maybe they'll camp not far from here and come in by mornin'," Wilkins said.

"Could be. Lieutenant, sit by the fire and have some coffee. I think we have enough bacon and beans for everyone."

Prince approached the fire, and the other men made room for him. Roper jerked his head at Dexter, and they walked a little ways off.

"I want you to ride down west of town and wait for Sally," he said. "If he's close enough to town, he'll keep riding through the dark 'til he gets here."

"That's what I figured," Dexter said. "Only why are we waitin' up here and not in town?"

Roper explained the situation, and Dexter ended up laughing.

"You got run out of town?"

"I did. I don't think it's so funny."

"Well, I do and so will Sally."

"Never mind," Roper said.

"How about if I go down to town and wait?" Dexter suggested. "Nobody there knows me."

"So many strangers in town too close together will be suspicious," Roper said. "If you ride in, then Sally and Hampstead ride in . . . no." He shook his head. "I've probably already attracted too much attention as it is. Let's do it my way."

"Hey," Dexter said, "you're the boss."

Dexter walked to his horse and mounted up as Roper walked to the fire.

"Where's he goin'?" Wilkins asked.

"He's going to wait for Bando and Hampstead outside of town," Roper said. "I don't want them riding in if they don't have to."

"Too much attention," Prince said.

"That's right."

"You might already have that problem," Prince said.

"What do you mean?"

"I stopped in a town earlier today, one that Dexter and Mr. Templeton bypassed."

"And?"

"The word is out that you gunned down three men in the street in Gilette."

"Already?"

"Yes, sir."

"Damn it," Roper said. "The killer is sure to hear that, or see it in a newspaper."

"It'll take him days to get here," Prince said.

"Depending on where he is when he sees it," Roper said. "We're going to have to leave here tomorrow."

"And go where?" Prince asked.

"Well," Roper said, looking around the fire, "after Sally Bando gets here with Hampstead and we talk about it, I think I'd like us all to go to Hurricane, West Virginia."

"And what's there?" Zack Templeton asked.

"Hopefully," Roper said, "answers."

54

Roper split the watch with Prince. He left
Wilkins and Templeton to sit off by themselves and discuss the situation.

"How much do you know?" he asked
Prince. They were sitting at the fire before
Prince turned in and Roper went on watch.

"About what?"

"About what's going on," Roper said.
"About why I was sent out here. About
whatever Victoria Westover and your boss
are keeping from me."

"Actually," Prince said, "I don't know
anything. I was just told to find you and
help you."

"White told you this?"

Prince nodded. "He's my boss."

"Why did Donny think you'd be able to
help me?" Roper asked.

"Donny?" Prince asked with a laugh.

"We go back a long way."

"I've never heard anybody call him

Donny."

"Let's get back to my question."

"Yes, well, I'm quite a good shot, very good with my hands —"

"A good tracker?"

"Fair," Prince said. "I have to admit that's not my strong suit, but if it comes to a fight, I'll be very helpful."

"Oh, it's going to come to a fight, all right," Roper said. "Somebody wants those three men dead."

"Who?"

"I'm not sure," Roper said, "but it might even be my own client, who sent me out to find them. If that's the case, I'm not going to be very happy. I don't like being used as a bird dog — especially without me knowing it."

"If someone wants them dead so bad," Prince asked, "why aren't they?"

"I don't know," Roper said. "I don't understand why three different killers weren't sent to kill each of them. Why was it done this way?"

"I can't help you, sir," Prince said.

"Well, somebody's got the answers," Roper said, "either in West Virginia or Washington." He shook his head. "This will teach me not to be soft."

"Soft?"

"A wounded war hero, an attractive wife, and I agree to go running around the country for weeks at a time. What was I thinking?"

At that moment they heard horses approaching, and then Dexter rode into camp, followed by Sally Bando and Dave Hampstead.

"Sally's here!" Bando shouted, announcing himself.

He dropped off his horse and shook hands with Roper.

"Good to see you, Sally."

"I got your man here, safe and sound."

"Anybody follow you?" Roper asked.

"Not that we saw," Bando said.

A man would have to be pretty damn good to follow Bando without him knowing it.

"Why? Somebody followed Dexter?"

"But I knew about it," Dexter said quickly.

Hampstead was shaking hands with Wilkins and Templeton, then came over and asked, "Are you Roper?"

"I am," Roper said.

"Do we get to find out what the hell's going on now?" Hampstead said.

"You do," Roper said. "Let's have some coffee and I'll explain."

"Got any food?" Bando asked.

"I think we've got some beans left in the

pot," Prince said.

"Who're you?" Bando asked.

"If everyone will gather around the fire," Roper called, "I'll make the last of the introductions and then explain."

As he made his explanations, the lights in the town below winked out a few at a time. When he was finished, the town was dark.

"Westover, huh?" Hampstead asked.

"Yes," Roper said.

"Well," Templeton said, "I'm not signin' nothin'. Not for Westover."

"Zack!" Hampstead said.

Roper looked from Templeton to Hampstead to Wilkins and asked, "What did I miss?"

Nobody answered.

"Okay, look," Roper said, "I'm tired of being in the dark. I want some answers."

The three men stared at him.

55

"Are you sure this is the way to play it?" Edward Harwick asked.

"Look, Mr. Lawyer," Kilkenny said. "You hired me to do this job, so you're gonna have to relax and let me do it my way."

"I can let you do it," Harwick said, "but relaxing won't be part of the deal."

"This is a good steak," Kilkenny said. "You got some fine restaurants in this town."

They were sitting across from each other in a Hurricane, West Virginia, steak house. When Harwick got the message that Kilkenny was in town, he was surprised. He met the hired killer at his hotel, and Kilkenny explained himself in part. Now, over steaks, he made his position clear.

"Once I heard Roper was in Gilette, Wyoming, and I realized Gilette was between Helena and Pierre, I knew what he was doing."

"What's that?" Harwick asked.

"Gathering the rest of the men on the list," Kilkenny responded.

"How do you know?"

"Because that's what I'd do," Kilkenny said. "Roper is supposed to be good."

"But what makes you think he'll bring them here?" Harwick asked.

"What else would he do with them?" Kilkenny asked. "Roper's gonna want some answers, and he's gonna want them from you, or from Mrs. Westover. For that he has to come here. And he'll bring them with him to keep them safe. Only, me and my men will be waiting for them."

"How many men did you bring with you?"

"I brought five reliable gunhands," Kilkenny said. "And when we got here, I hired some locals — not so reliable, but they know the lay of the land."

"When are you going to do it?"

"As soon as they get off the train," Kilkenny said. "You don't want Roper getting to the Westover house, and you sure as hell don't want him to get back to Washington, right?"

"That's right."

"Why didn't you just have him killed when he was here?"

"That wasn't the plan," Harwick said.

"Sending him after those men, and having them turn up dead one at a time, would point to him as the killer. It would look like he was a hired killer . . . like you."

"A man with Roper's rep?" Kilkenny said. "Why would you even take that chance? Why didn't you hire me in the first place — or somebody like me? Or when you did hire me, just let me kill him in Washington?"

"Look," Harwick said, "it's your job to do what you're paid to do, not to question the decisions."

Kilkenny stared across the table at the lawyer, who shifted uncomfortably beneath the killer's gaze, and finally looked away.

"The decisions?" he repeated. Then he smiled. "Oh, I get it. You're a hired hand, like me. You're not makin' the decisions."

"But I am paying for your dinner," Harwick pointed out.

"Yeah, that you are," Kilkenny said. He waved at a waiter. "I'm gonna have another steak."

56

"So this is what you were talking about when we were riding around the countryside on horseback?" Templeton asked Tommy Dexter.

Dexter was staring out the window at the scenery going by. He turned his head to look at Templeton and said, "Yeah, I like this a lot better than being on a horse."

"Not me. I like horses."

"Well," Templeton said, "I guess we're both gonna get our way, then."

Roper was in the stock car, checking on the horses. They had seven of them — one for him, Prince, Sally Bando, Tommy Dexter, and then Wilkins, Hampstead, and Templeton.

They all looked solid and fit. He dropped the sorrel's front foot and straightened up, thinking back to that night in camp when he'd demanded answers.

"I ain't ready to talk," Templeton had said.

"Me neither," Hampstead had agreed. "We don't know you from Adam, Roper."

Roper had looked at Wilkins. "You know me better than they do."

"But not that well," Wilkins had said. "I think what we oughta do is head to Hurricane and have this out with Westover."

"I don't know if he's in any shape to have anything out."

"His wife, then. She's the one who gave you our names, right?"

"That's right."

"Then we should talk to her," Templeton had said. "All of us. You'll get your answers then, Roper."

The men had been stubborn after that, and even as they'd traveled together over the next few days, they wouldn't talk. Oh, they'd sit together some nights when they camped, eat together, and talk among themselves, but around Roper and his men, not a word . . .

He came back to the present as Dave Hampstead entered the car.

"Dave."

"I have to talk to you, Roper."

"Sure. What's it about?"

"I think you know," Hampstead said. "I've

been a businessman for fifteen years now. Before this I hadn't been on a horse in a long time, and I haven't fired a gun for even longer."

Roper turned so he was facing the man squarely.

"You were a soldier."

"Yeah, twenty years ago," Hampstead said. "I won't do you any good when we get there, not with a gun."

"So what do you want to do?"

"I think I'd like to stay on the train."

"Okay," Roper said, "why don't you do that?"

"The other guys won't mind?"

"You know Wilkins and Templeton better than I do," Roper said.

"I haven't seen them for years," Hampstead said. "I don't know."

"All right, well, I'll square it with the rest of them."

"Will you? Thanks, Roper."

"Yeah."

Hampstead turned to leave, almost running into Sally Bando.

"What's wrong with him?" Bando asked.

"He's scared," Roper said. "Hasn't handled a gun since the war apparently."

"So what's he gonna do?"

"Stay on the train."

"Might as well," Bando said. "Wouldn't do us much good anyway, would he?"

"No, he wouldn't."

Roper patted the sorrel's neck.

"The horses are okay," he said. "You ready?"

"Me? I'm always ready. So's Tommy. What about that kid?"

"The lieutenant? He was okay in Washington. He'll be okay in Hurricane."

"And the other two?"

"They're not scared," Roper said. "They're okay. Hampstead's the only one, but like he says, he's been a businessman for the past fifteen years."

"Okay. The conductor says we should be pullin' into the station in about twenty minutes."

"All right," Roper said. "You help me bring the horses out."

Bando nodded.

"We got any idea who we're up against?" he asked.

"Killer for hire. That's all I know."

"Wish I knew who it was."

"Well," Roper said. "We'll find out soon enough."

57

The train pulled into the Hurricane, West Virginia, station. It was not a large station, and as people disembarked, the station started to get crowded with not only passengers, but the people who were greeting them.

"Here we go again," Lenny Sparr said to his partner, Mike Baker. This was the second train to arrive that day while they were waiting.

"What are we supposed to do?" Baker asked. "Stop everybody and ask 'em if their names is Talbot Roper? And what kinda name is that? Talbot?"

"We're lookin' for a bunch of men gettin' off the train together," his partner said. "Maybe gatherin' around the stock car to take some horses off. We'll know 'em when we see 'em."

"And where are the rest of the guys?" Baker asked. "Why's this all up to us?"

"They're across the street in the hotel," Sparr told him. "Kilkenny's there, too, unless he's havin' another steak."

"I ain't never seen anybody eat steak the way he does," Sparr said. "Why don't he weigh three hundred pounds?"

"He's a big man," Baker said with a shrug. "Maybe he does."

Sparr shook his head, watched as people got off the train.

"I don't like this," Baker said. "We don't know what we're doin'."

His friend laughed and asked, "Do we ever?"

They started to laugh and then Baker nudged Sparr and jerked his head. Sparr turned and saw Kilkenny entering the station, with the lawyer.

"Guess Kilkenny decided to greet Roper himself," Baker said.

"Come on," Sparr said. "We better look alive."

"This isn't right," Harwick said.

"You're the one who knows what Roper looks like," Kilkenny pointed out.

"But if he sees me with you —"

"He doesn't know who I am."

"What are we going to do?" Harwick asked. "Meet every train?"

"Starting today, yes," Kilkenny said. "Every train. They should be here today or tomorrow."

"How can you be sure?"

"Roper is a pro," Kilkenny said. "He'll be comin' here, and it shouldn't take him longer than today or tomorrow."

"How can you depend on that?"

"You can depend on a pro, my friend," Kilkenny said. "If he's as good as his rep, and I think he is."

Passengers started to get off the train. Kilkenny forgot about the lawyer.

Dave Hampstead got off the train and looked around. Roper told him what to do, how to act, and what to look for. By following his instructions, he noticed the men watching the train without being noticed himself. He was nervous, but he kept walking and got himself outside the station safely.

There was a hotel across the street from the station. Roper told him not to get a room there. Don't stay at the hotel nearest the station, or the next nearest. Get to the third one, and take a room there. Then rent a horse.

Roper wanted Hampstead to watch the station, spot the men who would probably be watching the trains. He'd already done that. Hampstead didn't think he had time to get a room at a hotel. Instead he went right to a livery and got a horse and buggy. When he got the buggy, he tossed his bag into it, then climbed aboard and snapped the reins at the single horse.

Roper had told Hampstead where they'd be riding into town. All he had to do was follow the directions. He was worried he'd get lost, but Roper's directions turned out to be perfect.

He reached the meeting point and reined the horse in. He lit a cigarette and settled down to wait, nervously — very nervously.

"Hampstead may make a mess of things," Sally said. "He's a bundle of nerves."

"He'll be okay," Roper said.

They were riding side by side, ahead of the others. They had all gotten off the train at the station before Hurricane and ridden the rest of the way. Roper was sure the station in town would be watched, so he took advantage of the fact that Hampstead had stayed on the train.

"He knows what to do when he gets to the station," Roper said.

"I don't like nervous people," Sally Bando said.

"Normally, neither do I, but I think Hampstead will be just nervous enough to be careful."

"Hope you're right."

Two hours later Roper was surprised to see a buggy up ahead of them. He expected to have to find Hampstead in a hotel. Instead the man was there, standing up in a buggy and waving.

"Well, well . . ." Sally said. "Look who's here."

When they reached him, Hampstead said quickly, "They're at the train station. I saw them!"

They surrounded him, remained astride their horses.

"Take it easy, Davey," Templeton said.

"Mr. Hampstead," Roper said, "calm down and tell me what you saw."

"Well, like you said, men, and all they were doing was . . . watching. They weren't waiting for anyone, or waiting for the train. They were just . . . watching."

"How many did you see?"

Hampstead hesitated, then said, "Four."

"If they were equals, they'd all be looking at the trains, and the people. If one of them was the boss, they'd be stealing glances at him."

"That makes sense," Hampstead said. "They were looking at this big man — tall, broad shoulders, lots of red hair . . ."

"Pale skin?" Roper asked. "Big knobby hands?"

"Yeah, that's him."

"Boss?" Sally said.

Roper looked at Bando, and Dexter.

"Kilkenny," Roper said.

"Jesus," Dexter said.

"Who's Kilkenny?" Hampstead asked.

"A killer for hire," Sally said. "Big rep. If he's after you, you're dead."

Hampstead swallowed hard and sat down.

"Have you ever seen him?" Dexter asked Roper.

"Seen him, yes, met him, no."

"Gone up against him?" Templeton asked.

"No," Roper said, then, "not yet."

"What do we do now?" Hampstead asked.

"Go to town?" Wilkins asked.

"Go to the station?" Templeton suggested.

"No!" Hampstead said.

Roper looked at them.

"I have a better idea," he said.

"What's that?" Wilkins asked.

"You three want to see your old comrade, Howard Westover?"

58

Roper led them all to the Westover house, including Dave Hampstead in his rented buggy. He dismounted and looked at Sally Bando.

"You and Dex stay out here."

"Rifles?"

"Yes."

Bando and Dexter took their rifles from their saddles, walked up onto the porch, and took up position at either end.

Roper went to the front door with Wilkins, Templeton, and Hampstead.

"What about me?" Prince asked.

"Cover the back."

"Yessir."

As the young lieutenant went around the back, Roper knocked on the door. When the door opened, Victoria Westover was standing there.

"Mr. Roper," she said. "What are you doing here?" She looked beyond him. "And who are these men?"

"These are three of the men," he said, "that you hired Sean Kilkenny to kill."

She stared at him for a few seconds, then said, "You'd better come in, then."

Victoria led the four men into the living room, then turned to face them.

"I don't know what you're talking about. Who are these men?"

"This is Henry Wilkins, Dave Hampstead, and Zack Templeton," Roper said, making the introductions. "Men, this is Victoria Westover, your old buddy's wife." He looked at her again. "These are three of the men whose names were on the list you gave me. Gerald Quinn was dead when I reached him, killed by your man. Vince McCord had died many years ago. You lucked out there."

"I still don't know —"

"What I'm talking about, I know," he said. "That's why I'm telling you. You told me these men would sign affidavits to the effect that your husband earned his Medal of Honor. Well, they're not signing. Do you know why? They don't know anything about your husband being wounded in the war."

She stared at him.

"Why the lies, Mrs. Westover?" he asked. "Why set these men up to be killed, and why would you want me to find them dead?

Why send me traipsing around the country for weeks — months — for apparently no reason?"

"I'm afraid that was my doing," a voice said.

They all looked toward the doorway, saw a man standing there with a gun in his hand.

It was Howard Westover.

"Now why doesn't this surprise me?" Roper asked.

"This is wrong," Kilkenny suddenly said.

"What do you mean?" Harwick asked.

"I've been stupid," the killer said. "Roper's not comin' in on the train."

"Why do you say that?"

"Because I wouldn't," Kilkenny said.

"But you said —"

"I know what I said," Kilkenny said, cutting him off, "but I've changed my mind."

"Why?"

"Because I would suspect — and expect — an ambush at the train station."

"So then what is he doing?" the lawyer asked.

Kilkenny thought a moment, then said, "He got off the station before this and is ridin' in the rest of the way with the men. He might have even sent one man in by train to check out the station."

"To go where?"

"I've got to get my men," Kilkenny said, ignoring him. "Come on!"

"Where?"

Moving away from Harwick, Kilkenny said over his shoulder, "To see your client."

59

Actually, Roper was surprised to see Westover up on his feet, holding a gun, only because the man had seemed so frail when he'd last seen him. But the fact that there was a double cross like this didn't surprise him at all.

"I thought he was flat on his back, dyin'," Wilkins said.

"I guess that's what we were supposed to think," Roper said.

Victoria Westover walked to her husband and placed her hand on his chest.

"Let's get the word from the man himself," Roper said. "Why do you want all these men dead, Howard?"

Westover didn't answer, and his three colleagues all looked away.

"Wait a minute," Roper said, looking around. "How stupid am I? I'm the only one who doesn't know the answer, right?"

"Put the gun down, Howard," Templeton

said. "You can't get all of us."

"I can get some of you," Westover said. Watching him, Roper could see that the man was indeed ill; he just wasn't as close to death's door as they wanted him to think.

"What did you all do?" Roper asked. "During the war. What happened?"

"Well," Wilkins said, "for one thing, it was Gerry Quinn who gave Westover that festering wound."

"I'm glad, at least, that he's dead," Victoria said, standing beside her man. The hand holding the gun was not steady, and she seemed to be adding to her husband's strength.

There was so much tension in the air, it felt like electricity. Templeton was wearing a gun on his hip; Wilkins and Hampstead were both holding rifles. At any moment the air could be filled with hot lead, and Roper was ready to hit the floor if that happened. Obviously, there was no love lost between Westover and these men.

"You boys better put those rifles down," Westover said.

"I don't think so," Templeton said.

"Then somebody's going to die today," Westover said.

"Now hold on," Roper said. "Before you fellas start killing each other — or me — I want to know what this is all about."

Westover, his wife, and the other three men all exchanged glances.

"Wow," Roper said. "Whatever it is, it's a big secret. Even now, with two of you dead and the rest of you about to shoot each other, you don't want to talk about it."

Roper decided to speak directly to Howard Westover.

"Why do I think this is partly about you losing your medal?"

"Medal," Westover said dismissively. "What good does a medal do anyone?"

Roper wondered if he was so in the dark that everyone, including even Donald White in Washington, knew what had really gone on among these men.

Outside Sally Bando walked over to Tommy Dexter and asked, "You see what I see?"

"Yeah," Dexter sad. "Dust cloud. Better go inside and let the boss know."

Bando nodded and went to the door. When he tried to open it, it wouldn't budge.

"Door's locked," he said.

"Knock on it!"

Bando knocked, then knocked again more insistently.

"We're locked out," he said, trying the doorknob again, "and I don't like it."

"These riders are gettin' closer," Dexter said. "See if you can find a window that'll let you see what the hell is goin' on."

In the rear of the house, Prince decided nobody was going to come running out the back. He started to move around to the side of the house, hoping to see inside. In doing so, he ran into Bando.

"What's goin' on?" he asked.

"Riders comin'," Bando said. "I'm tryin' to tell Roper, but the front door is locked. How about the back?"

"Locked, too."

"You better go to the front and stand with Dex," Bando said.

"Right."

As Prince continued on to the front of the house, Bando looked at the window in front of him, said, "Aw, shit," took his gun from his holster, and used it to smash the glass.

At the sound of the breaking window, Westover's finger tightened on the trigger and he fired off a shot. Everyone ducked and went for his own gun, or brought up his rifle.

"Stop! Stop!" Roper shouted, waving his hands.

Everybody froze.

"Roper?"

The detective said, "That's my man. Sally! In here!"

Bando appeared behind Westover, one of his hands bloody, the other holding his gun. He reacted immediately and stuck his gun in Westover's back.

"Drop it."

Westover dropped his gun, and then slumped to the floor. It was as if all his strength was in that gun.

"Howard," Victoria said. Unable to hold him up, she went to the floor with him.

"What happened?" Roper asked Bando.

"Riders comin'. Lots of them, judging from the amount of dust they're kickin' up. The front door was locked so I had to break a window to get in."

"You all right?"

"Yeah, just a cut. Who's this jasper?" He indicated Westover.

"Our host," Roper said.

"I don't understand," Bando said. "I thought he was dyin'."

"So did I." Roper looked at the other three. "I still don't know what's going on, but we better get outside."

"All right," Templeton said, while Hampstead and Wilkins nodded.

"What about Howard?" Victoria said.

321

"You can't leave him here."

The three ex–Union soldiers looked down at their former colleague, then stepped over him to get outside.

Roper looked down at Victoria and said, "Right now, this is probably the safest place for him."

Before he left the room, he picked up Westover's gun.

Outside, Roper felt like an ass.

Not only was he now in a position to be in a huge firefight, but he had gotten Bando and Dex into the same position. All because he had made a bad decision, based not only on Westover's condition and his wife's pleas, but on the money she was paying as well.

"What's wrong, boss?" Bando asked.

"I'm sorry I got you — uh — into this."

"What the hell," Bando said. "We all gotta do it sometime."

Leave it to Sally Bando to put it all in its proper context.

60

When Kilkenny came within sight of the house, he reined his horse in. His men followed.

"What's wrong?" Harwick asked. He was astride a horse for the first time in a long time.

"On the porch," Kilkenny said. "They saw us comin'."

"Whataya wanna do, boss?" Eric Striker asked. Striker was Kilkenny's number two.

The killer turned in his saddle. He had about thirteen men with him, not counting the lawyer. On the porch he counted about half as many.

"Eric, take half the men and circle around. I want you to come from the back."

"When do we go?"

"When you hear the first shot," Kilkenny said. "I'm gonna ride up to the house and talk to Roper."

"What for?" Harwick asked.

"Well," Kilkenny said, "for one thing, I wanna meet him."

"What the hell —" Dexter said.

"What is it?" Roper said. He had just come out the door with Templeton, Wilkins, and Hampstead behind him.

"One rider coming, sir," Prince said.

"That's a big man," Bando said.

"Yeah," Roper said. "Kilkenny."

As the rider came closer, Roper could see his pale skin and red hair and knew that this was the hired killer, Sean Kilkenny.

"You wouldn't happen to know this fella, would you?" Roper asked Prince.

"No, sir. Why would you think that?"

"Wouldn't be the first time the Secret Service employed a killer to do their dirty work for them."

"Well, sir, as far as I know, that's not the case this time."

Kilkenny rode right up to them and reined in.

"Talbot Roper?"

"That's me," the detective said.

"You're pretty good," Kilkenny said. "Took me a while to figure out you wouldn't be on the train."

"And now that you've got it figured?"

"Well, I've got a job to do," Kilkenny said.

"Yeah," Roper said, "you're getting paid to kill these three."

"That's true," Kilkenny said, "but my job don't include these other three. You fellas can mount up and ride out."

"You'd like that, wouldn't you?" Roper said. "That'd leave just the four of us."

"That's okay," Bando said to Kilkenny. "I'll stay."

"Me, too," Dexter said.

"And me," Prince added.

"You're outnumbered," Kilkenny pointed out.

"So what do you expect us to do, just sit here and let you kill us?" Roper asked. "We'll take some of you sons of bitches with us."

"Probably you among 'em," Bando said.

Kilkenny looked at the seven men on the porch. He knew Hampstead wouldn't be much good with the rifle, but the other six were probably competent.

"Well, don't say I didn't give you a chance."

"Whataya got, a dozen men?" Bando asked.

"More than that."

"That's okay," Dexter said. "We're ready."

"Got your boss inside," Roper said.

"That a fact?"

"We could make sure nobody's around to pay you," the detective said. "Then you'd be risking your life for nothing."

"I start a job, I finish it," Kilkenny said. "I got half my money up front."

Damn, Roper thought, they had to run into a killer who had pride in his work.

"Well," Kilkenny said, "I'll give you boys some time to think it over before we come in. Mr. Roper, it was a pleasure meetin' you."

"Mr. Kilkenny," Roper said, "you got that lawyer out there with you?"

"Yes, sir, I do."

"Why don't you send him on in?" Roper said. "We'll let him talk to Mr. and Mrs. Westover, and maybe we can solve this without bloodshed."

"Well, sir," Kilkenny said, "I wouldn't mind that as long as I still got paid. I'll send him on in."

"Thank you."

"I kill for money, Mr. Roper," Kilkenny said. "There's nothin' personal in it."

"I understand."

"I thought you would."

Kilkenny wheeled his horse around and rode back to his men.

61

"Prince?"

"Yes, sir?"

"Take Templeton and go and have a look in the back."

"You thinkin' he's gonna split his men into two groups?" Bando asked. "Come in from behind?"

"That's what I'd do."

"Come on," Prince said to Templeton, and the two of them went around to the back of the house.

"You really think that lawyer fella is gonna come ridin' in here?" Bando asked.

"I think if Kilkenny tells him to, he will."

"You two got yourselves a little admiration society there, don't ya?"

"I respect a man who's good at his job," Roper said, "even if that job is killing."

"You believe that young soldier that Kilkenny ain't workin' for the government?"

"I believe that he believes he's not."

"You want me to what?" Harwick asked.

"Ride in there and talk to Roper."

"B-But . . . he knows I'm with you?"

"He does."

"How?"

"Well, I told him."

"What?"

"He asked if you were with me, and I said yes."

"Why did you do that?"

"There wasn't no reason to lie," Kilkenny said. "So go on, ride in."

"I — I can't."

"You can, and you will," Kilkenny said. "I said you would."

"I think I should go back to —"

Kilkenny cut him off. "Don't make me tie you to your horse and send you in there. Besides, you'll want to talk to your clients. Roper wants to try and settle this with no bloodshed."

"And you're okay with that?"

"As long as I get paid," Kilkenny said. "I'm not bloodthirsty, lawyer, but I am money hungry. Now go!"

The lawyer swallowed hard, but he knew Kilkenny was serious. He would tie him to his saddle.

Harwick started his horse moving toward the house, briefly considered making a run for it, but he didn't relish the thought of both Kilkenny and Roper being after him.

He maintained his course and rode for the house.

"Here he comes," Bando said.

"And he don't look happy," Dexter added.

"Sally," Roper said, "why don't you go inside and see how our hosts are doing?"

"Yes, sir."

Bando went inside as Harwick reached them.

"Y-You, uh, wanted to talk to me?" he asked Roper.

"Don't be nervous, Harwick," Roper said. "I'm always suspicious of lawyers, and I was always suspicious of you. So you've done nothing to surprise or disappoint me."

"Um, all right," Harwick said. "What do you want with me now?"

Bando came out of the house. "They're right where we left them."

"Mr. Westover is still alive?"

"Yes, sir."

Roper looked at the lawyer.

"Dismount, Harwick."

"Uh —"

"You heard the man," Bando said. "Dismount before I drag you down."

Harwick hurriedly dismounted, wondering why everybody was threatening him. He'd only been doing his job all along.

"Go inside and talk to your clients," Roper said. "Tell them to call off their killer, and pay him off in full. It's all over. There's no reason for anyone else to die."

Harwick started to put his foot on the first step, then hesitated.

"Well, go ahead," Roper said. "Nobody's going to stop you."

He came up the steps warily, eyeing the men and their guns, and then went into the house.

"Hopefully," Roper said, "by the time he comes out, this will all be over — as far as Kilkenny's concerned, that is."

62

Harwick walked into the house and saw Victoria Westover sitting on the floor next to her prone husband.

Her dead husband.

She looked up at Harwick and said, "He stopped breathing about a minute ago."

"Victoria —"

"I want them all dead, Edward," she said, tears streaming down her face. "I want them all dead, do you understand?"

"Yes," he said. "Yes, I understand, but —"

She stood up and got right in his face.

"I don't know why they sent you in here," she said, "but you go out and tell them they're all going to die. And you tell Kilkenny I want them all dead."

"Victoria —"

"I will double his fee."

"I don't know —"

"And I'll double yours."

He studied her face and knew there was

no talking her out of it.

When Harwick came out, Roper looked at him.

"Well?"

"Mr. Westover is dead."

"Well, that's too bad," Roper said. He looked at the others. Wilkins and Hampstead didn't look all broken up about it.

"What about Victoria?" Roper asked.

"She wants you all dead," the lawyer said. "She said she'll double Kilkenny's fee — and mine."

"Is that a fact?"

"And I guess you didn't try to talk her out of it, did you?" Bando asked.

"I did try," Harwick said. "It was no use."

Roper looked at the three Civil War vets and asked, "Doesn't Westover being dead end it? Huh?"

They stared back at him, but before one of them could answer, Dexter said, "Whatever it means to them, it ain't over for Kilkenny. Not as long as she's gonna pay — and double!"

"But he doesn't know that," Roper said. "He doesn't know she's going to pay him double, does he?"

"Well," Harwick said, "I have to go back and tell him. He's expecting me."

"No," Roper said.

"What? But . . . I have to."

"No, you don't," Roper said.

"He'll kill me —"

"If you try to get on that horse, I'll kill you," Roper said.

"But if I don't tell him," Harwick said, "he'll just ride in and kill us all."

"He'll try," Dexter said.

"I can't — I'm not good in a fight."

"Just go over there and sit down," Roper said. "Over there against the wall. And don't move."

"But —"

"Do it!"

Harwick walked up to the house and sat down on the porch with his back against the wall.

"So what do we do now, boss?" Bando asked.

"I'll do what Kilkenny did," Roper said. "I'll ride up to him and tell him Westover's dead and there's nobody to pay him."

"That'll make him mad," Hampstead said, "won't it?"

Roper, Dexter, and Bando didn't pay any attention to him.

"You can see how many men he's got, too," Bando said.

"However many men he lets me see,"

Roper said, "he'll have double."

"That's the formula," Dexter said.

"All right," Roper said. "That's what I'll do. The rest of you wait here, watch for any surprises. Dex, you better go in the back and tell Prince and Templeton to stay alert."

"Okay, boss. You be careful."

"Kilkenny's a pro," Roper said. "He'll give me the same courtesy I gave him."

"I hope you're right," Bando said.

Roper walked to his palomino and mounted up.

"Boss."

Kilkenny didn't look at Fergus, the man who had spoken, but he said, "I see him."

"When he gets here," Fergus said, "we can kill him. That'll leave them without a leader."

"If you touch your gun while he's here, I'll kill you myself, Fergus. Understand?"

"No."

"That's okay," Kilkenny said. "Just so long as you hear me."

"I hear you."

"Good. Pass the word. Nobody touches their gun while he's here."

"Okay, boss."

Kilkenny watched Roper approach and waited.

■ ■ ■ ■

"He's what?" Kilkenny asked.

"Dead," Roper said. "Westover died."

"Well, shit. Why didn't that lawyer come back and tell me that?"

"I told him to stay at the house. I figured I'd tell you myself."

While Kilkenny digested the information, Roper looked at his men. There were six of them. That meant there were at least six he couldn't see, maybe more. Kilkenny had said he had more than a dozen, but there was no telling how many more. Roper was going to have to figure a dozen as a minimum.

"So what do you think we do now, Roper?" Kilkenny asked.

"Well, I've got an idea," Roper said. "But I don't know if you're going to like it."

"Try me."

Roper looked at him and said, "Why don't we all go home?"

63

Roper rode back to the house and dismounted.

"What'd he say?" Bando asked.

"He's coming in," Roper said.

"Jesus," Harwick said, burying his head in his hands.

"Hey, lawyer," Roper said, "you might as well go inside."

He didn't have to be told twice. He got to his feet and ran inside.

"Let's spread out," Roper said.

"Boss, there should be more than two of us in the back," Dexter said.

"I agree, Dex, but why don't you get up on the roof somehow. Maybe you can move freely up there."

"Right."

Dex went inside.

"All right, the rest of us better spread out, make every shot count. If we fire accurately, we can turn a superior group."

"How do we play this, boss?" Fergus asked.
"We kill everybody there but the lady who's payin' the bills," Kilkenny said. "Got it?"
"Got it, boss."
"Let the men know."
"Yep." He started away.
"And Fergus?"
He stopped. "Yeah?"
"You're leadin' the men in."
"Yes, sir!"
Fergus hurried off to relay the orders to the men.
Kilkenny was going to go in last, to mop up. He doubted his men would be able to get Roper. That would be his job.
He settled back to watch.

"Why is he still comin' in?" Bando asked Roper. "Didn't you tell him the man payin' the bills is dead?"
"I told him."
"And?"
"It didn't seem to bother him."
"Why the hell not?"
Roper looked at him. "My guess is it wasn't Mr. Westover who was paying him."
Bando looked surprised. "Mrs. Westover

337

hired him?"

"Apparently."

"And now she wants us all dead."

"Yep."

Bando shook his head. "Mean lady."

"Here they come!" Wilkins said.

Roper saw them, riding abreast with their guns drawn.

"They're making a mistake already," he said.

"Handguns," Bando said.

"Right."

"What?" Hampstead asked.

"They need to get close."

Bando tossed Roper a rifle, brandished his own. Hampstead and Wilkins were already holding theirs.

"There's only four of us," Hampstead said.

"Seven coming at us," Roper said, "probably more in the back."

"There's only three of us back there," Hampstead pointed out.

"That's why we have to start firing first," Roper said.

"First?" Hampstead said.

"Now!"

They opened fire.

Kilkenny watched and shook his head. To

think that he should have had to tell his men to use their rifles made him sad. He'd had to hire too many locals, and they were idiots. He hoped that Striker would know better when he and his men came in from the back.

In addition, the old soldiers were firing their weapons with entirely too much accuracy. He had been led to believe that they had hardly touched guns since the war.

As he watched his men fly from their saddles as if plucked by an invisible hand, he decided he was going to have to settle for the first half of his payment. It was his own damn fault. He'd known about Roper from the beginning. He should have made sure he had more reliable men. He wouldn't make that same mistake again.

He was going to have to run away to face Roper another day. But not until he checked on Striker's progress.

Roper and the men on the porch were able to fire many times before any of Kilkenny's men got close enough for their pistols to pose a danger. By the time a few bullets struck the house and broke some windows, most of the men were on the ground. In the end there were only two left, and they turned their horses and rode off as a hail of bullets continued to come from the porch.

"Sally!" Roper shouted. "Take Wilkins and get to the back of the house!"

"Right, boss."

Roper remained on the porch with Hampstead, just in case another wave of men came, but that didn't happen. He heard gunfire from the back and hoped they were having as much success there as he'd had in front.

And then it was quiet.

64

Kilkenny circled around to the back. Striker and his men had apparently been smart enough to use their rifles, but they were still riding in on men who were firing from cover and, once again, with way too much accuracy.

This job was a mess. Kilkenny had learned a valuable lesson here. Too much money can make you ask not enough questions.

Striker came riding up to him while the battle was winding down.

"Boss, this ain't right. I thought we were facing men who —"

"I know," Kilkenny said, cutting him off. "We didn't get all the information we needed, Striker."

"So what do we do, boss?"

"This job is over," Kilkenny said.

"What about Roper?"

"He's a worthy opponent," Kilkenny said. "There'll be another day."

And with that, the two gunmen turned their horses and rode away as, behind them, the sound of shooting ceased . . .

Bando came back to the front of the house and said to Roper, "All over, boss. Looks like Kilkenny's gone."

"That was too easy," Roper said.

"Well, Prince took a bullet in the shoulder," Bando pointed out, "and Templeton got nicked on the arm."

"Anybody else hurt?"

"No."

Slowly, the other men came back around to the front of the house. Wilkins was letting Prince lean on him, and he set the Secret Service man down on the porch steps. Roper took a look at the wound.

"You'll be okay."

"Yes, sir," Prince said, wincing. "It's not too bad."

"I'm going to go inside and talk to Mrs. Westover," Roper said. "Keep an eye out, in case Kilkenny decides to get sneaky, but I really think he decided to cut his losses. His men weren't very smart to come riding in with their pistols in their hands instead of rifles."

"Can't get good help these days," Sally Bando said.

"Tell me about it," Roper said and went inside.

In the living room Victoria was still sitting on the floor next to her husband's body. The lawyer, Harwick, was standing off to the side with a large glass of brandy.

"It's over," Roper said. "Your killer gave up."

She turned her tear-streaked face up to him.

"If you think it's over, you're a fool."

"I am a fool," Roper said. "I was a fool to ever take this on, considering how many lies I was told. And I don't appreciate being set up to take the rap for what was supposed to be five murders."

Victoria looked at him and said, "I'll die before I tell you anything."

"Harwick," Roper said. "You want to talk? Fill in the gaps for me?"

"Believe me, Mr. Roper," Harwick said, "there are just as many gaps for me as well. I was just doing what I was told."

The man was leaving out the fact that he was in love with his client's wife. He'd no doubt been hoping the husband would finally die, perhaps unaware that the man hadn't been quite as close to death's door as his wife had been letting everyone believe.

However, it seemed as if the final effort it took him to get out of bed and come downstairs had done him in.

A goddamned mess that couldn't get any worse, Roper thought, only to be surprised again in the next few minutes.

65

Roper heard some activity behind him, turned to see Bando and Dexter walking into the room. They had no guns, and their hands were up.

"What the —" he said.

"Sorry, boss," Bando said. "They got the drop on us."

"Who?" Roper asked.

Entering the room behind them were Wilkins, Hampstead, and Templeton, who didn't seem much bothered by that nick in his left arm. All three of them were pointing their guns at Bando and Dexter.

"Now what the hell is going on?" Roper demanded. "Where's Prince?"

"Unconscious on the porch," Bando said.

"Sorry about this, Roper," Wilkins said. "You saved my life, but there's too much history here."

"What history?" Roper asked. "Do I get to hear what you all did at the end of the war that led to this?"

"Afraid not," Templeton said. He looked at Victoria. "Mrs. Westover, you know what we want. You know what your husband owed us."

"He didn't owe you anything!" she spat back. "If it wasn't for him, none of you would have had a thing. How did you repay him? You tried to kill him. I'll tell you nothing."

"And we did kill him," Hampstead pointed out, "if he finally died from that wound Quinn gave him."

"Okay, I think I'm getting it," Roper said. "You guys pulled a job at the end of the war, didn't you? Stole . . . what? Silver? Gold? Union or Confederate? Not that it matters."

"It's time for you to shut up, Roper," Dave Hampstead said.

"Bold talk for a businessman," Roper said. "And you handled your rifle pretty well out there, Hampstead. Guess you're not the tenderfoot you want people to believe you turned into."

"Time to get rid of your gun, Roper," Templeton said.

"You three are worried about one man with a gun?"

"Don't make me kill you," Templeton said.

"Why not? You're going to kill us anyway, aren't you?" Roper asked. "And then search the house for what you want?"

"They c-can't do that!" Harwick blubbered.

"Shut up!" Hampstead snapped. "Drop your gun."

Roper noticed some movement behind them, so he said, "No."

"Damn it!" Hampstead said, raising his rifle.

"Wait —" Wilkins said. He'd come to know Roper better than the other two, and perhaps had some qualms about killing him, but Roper would never know. Prince had crept into the house behind them, bleeding from the shoulder, but holding his pistol in his hand.

"Drop 'em!" he shouted.

Surprised by the voice behind them, all three men started to turn. Roper went for his gun. Bando and Dexter hit the floor to get out of the way. Too late the men realized their mistake. Two of them started to turn back, but Roper fired twice, Prince fired once. Of the three men, only Templeton pulled his trigger, but he fired into the floor. The three of them went down, and Bando and Dexter were on them quickly, kicking their guns away just in case.

Roper's two men checked the bodies. Roper looked past them at Prince, who was on the floor now, but conscious. He waved a hand at Roper to let him know he was all right.

"They're dead, boss," Bando said.

Roper looked around. Harwick was slumped against the wall, his hand on his bloody shoulder. He was alive, but he wasn't any good to anyone.

Victoria Westover was draped over her husband's body. He went to her, turned her over just enough to see that she had taken a bullet in the chest. She was as dead as her husband.

"Well, damn it!" Roper said, standing. "Now who do I get my answers from?"

66

Roper walked into Donald White's office and looked around at the furnishings. Quite different from the empty room he'd been in during his prior trip to Washington. This one had walls lined with bookshelves and cabinets and hung with photos of White and certain Washington dignitaries. His desk was large and utilitarian, the chairs plain and functional. Everything fit Donny White's personality perfectly. There was one window behind him, which looked out onto the White House in the distance.

"So this is your real office?" he asked. "This time I rate?"

"Sit down, Roper," White said. "You've got a right to be upset. By the way, thanks for bringing young Prince back. He's doing fine."

"He was helpful," Roper admitted, taking a seat, "so I thought I'd bring him back to you slightly battered, but in one piece."

"I appreciate it. Would you like a drink?"

"No, I don't want a drink, Donny," Roper said. "I want answers. What did Howard Westover and his friends do at the end of the war that led to all this death twenty years later? Why did you lie to me about the records being lost?"

"Roper," White said, "you know I can't tell you everything. Unless, of course, you want to come to work for me. Once you have the right clearance —"

"Oh, no," Roper said, "you're not going to blackmail me into joining the Secret Service. I did my time with Allan, I'm not going to serve under you."

"Well, then," White said, spreading his hands, "I'm afraid you're going to have to live with having a few gaps in the story."

"A few gaps?" Roper repeated. "That's what you call it?"

"You know," Donald White said, "you could have tried to get a few more answers from your client before you took the job."

Roper made a face and said, "Don't remind me. I know I got myself in a mess in the first place."

"Yes, you did."

Roper sat forward in his chair.

"That doesn't mean I have to stay in the dark."

"Settle back," White said. "Suppose you tell me what you think was going on."

"We making a game of it?"

"It was no game, was it, Tal?"

"I think Westover and his men pulled some kind of a job, then fell out. Gerald Quinn put a bullet into Westover, but they all ended up going their way with their share of the proceeds."

"And?"

"And for some reason, Westover got a Medal of Honor out of it."

"Seems to me that would make the others pretty dissatisfied."

"Yeah, but they couldn't say anything without incriminating themselves," Roper went on. "Now, years later, the government decides they want to recall some medals. Westover's is one of them. I'm thinking you suspected him of something at the end of the war, but couldn't prove it. What I can't figure is, why try to take his medal away after all this time, and him being sick."

White shrugged and said, "Maybe his name was just on the list."

"Then you hear I've been called in, and you think I'm going to come up with the proof, make it easy to take the medal and maybe even prosecute him. A last-ditch effort to solve the mystery of the missing . . . what?"

"We didn't know exactly who you were working for," White said, "but then neither did you, right?"

"Westover was sick," Roper said, "but not as sick as they let on. And then those other three . . ."

"Tal, you were trying to save their lives," White said. "I never figured they'd turn on you."

"Sure you did," Roper said, "that's why you sent Prince."

"I didn't know anything about Kilkenny's involvement," White said.

"You're supposed to know things like that, Donny," Roper said. "Maybe you messed up, too."

"Maybe I did."

"You know what?" Roper said. "I think I'll have that drink now."

White got up, went to a sideboard, opened it, and poured out two snifters of brandy.

"I thought you said a drink," Roper said, accepting the glass.

"Here on Capital Hill we drink brandy," White said, seating himself behind his desk again.

"All the more reason I should stay away

from Washington," Roper said, but he drank it.

"So they're all dead?" White said.

"All of them," Roper said. "There was a lot of lead flying around. Prince was lucky he just got winged."

"Not a very satisfying ending, is it?" White asked.

"No," Roper said. "I still don't know why I had to end up killing three men who fought in the war on the same side I did."

"You never get all the answers, Tal," White said. "You should know that in your business."

"I do know that," Roper said. "That doesn't mean I have to like it."

"Even the best can still learn something."

Roper stood up.

"Want to have a steak tonight?" White asked.

"I'm leaving on the next train," Roper said. "I've had enough of Washington to last me awhile."

"Well, it was good to see you."

"Hopefully, it'll be a long time before we see each other again, Donny," Roper said, then added, "No offense."

White laughed. "None taken."

At the door Roper stopped and asked, "How's it look for the colonel to get that third bird?"

"Not good," White said. "The old gent died last week."

"Too bad," Roper said, even though he and the colonel were never more than cordial with each other. "So he never had a part in any of this?"

"No, no," White said, "we were just trying to keep him out of trouble. According to Captain Morressy, the old man heard you were in town and just wanted to act like he still had some authority. I heard you went easy on him."

"I never liked him," Roper said, "but I always respected him. And he wasn't that aggressive. It was just kind of . . . sad."

"Well," White said, "hopefully we won't end up like that when we get old."

"Nothing worse than an old soldier without a war," Roper said.

"Amen," White said as Roper went out the door.

Outside Roper found Lieutenant Prince waiting for him, his left arm in a sling.

"How you feeling, son?" Roper asked.

"I'm fine, sir. I wanted to thank you for bringing me back here."

"And we owe you thanks for dragging yourself back into that house. You pretty much saved all our asses."

"It was sort of insulting to be ignored that way, sir."

"Well, you made damn sure you weren't ignored for very long," Roper said. "Good luck with your next assignment, whatever it is."

"Before you go, I thought this might interest you sir," Prince said.

He handed Roper a rolled-up file.

"What is it?"

"It's the file on an investigation that took place at the end of the war," Prince said. "Might be some interesting reading on the train back to Denver. Just don't tell anyone where you got it."

Roper watched the young man walk away, wondering if in his hand he was holding his answers after all.

EPILOGUE

Two months later . . .

The Westover case still left a bad taste in Roper's mouth. That was why he found his present job more palatable, a simple manhunt. No secrets here. He was tracking John Sender again, as he had been months before the Westover case. He'd returned Sender to the custody of the Colorado State Penitentiary, and had promptly forgotten about him until, a month after he'd returned from Washington, D.C., he was notified that Sender had once again escaped . . .

He was in his office at the time, trying to show another of Mrs. Batchelder's girls how to file. This one's name was Holly. She was a tall, willowy brunette who had the biggest doe eyes he'd ever seen, and the smallest waist.

The door opened and a man stepped into the office.

"Roper."

Roper and Holly both turned from their filing and looked at him.

"What do you want, Evans? Why'd they let you out of the pen?"

"I'm the assistant warden, Roper," Mike Evans said. "I can leave anytime I want."

"I was hoping maybe they'd gotten smart and decided to keep you inside. Holly, this is Mike Evans. If he ever comes by again, tell him I'm not in."

"Uh, yes, sir."

"All right, Evans," Roper said. "Let's go into my office."

He turned and went in, leaving Evans to follow him.

Roper didn't like Evans. The man had come up through the ranks, having been a deputy sheriff and a deputy marshal, and now, in his early forties, he was next in line to be the warden at the penitentiary, when the current warden retired in a year or so. But as far as Roper was concerned, he'd never been a good lawman. Rather, Evans was a politician and knew the right palms to grease and asses to kiss. He even dressed like a politician, in an expensive charcoal gray suit that was cut perfectly to fit.

"I'm not going to offer you a drink," Roper said. "I sense you won't be here long.

In fact, don't even sit down."

"You're right," Evans said. "I'm only here to tell you that Sender's out."

"You let him out?" Roper asked incredulously.

"No," Evans said, "we didn't let him out. He escaped."

"Again?"

"Look," Evans said, "he had help. He was assigned to the laundry — never mind. The details don't matter. We need you to bring him back."

"You've got marshals for that."

"You know him better than anyone. You've already caught him twice."

"I don't work for free, Evans."

"The state won't pay you, Roper, you know that," Evans said.

"Well then —"

"But I will."

"You?"

"Just send me the bill when you get back."

"Wait a minute," Roper said. "You made a mess of this, didn't you? He escaped on your watch."

"I need you to bring him back, Roper," Evans said. "What's it gonna take?"

"Well," Roper said, "for starters, double my usual fee . . . up front, of course . . ."

■ ■ ■ ■

He'd been tracking Sender for a couple of weeks and was closing in once again. Third time is the charm, he thought. Maybe this time when he put him away, he'd stay put. Or maybe this time he'd have to kill him.

He'd already tracked the two men who had helped Sender escape. He'd had to kill one — Charlie Wills — and he'd turned the other one — Larry Billings — over to the law. By now, Billings was in the pen himself, waiting for his buddy Sender to come back. Roper was doing his best to make that happen.

Billings had spilled to Roper that Sender was heading for Saint Joe, Missouri. Roper had been in Saint Joe during the Westover thing, so when he arrived, he stopped in to see Sheriff Parnell.

"What brings you back here?" Parnell asked as they shook hands.

"I'm tracking a man who escaped from the Denver pen," Roper said. "John Sender."

"I never heard of him. What's he look like?"

Roper described Sender — tall, broadshouldered, forty, with black hair — but didn't know if he'd have his silver-plated

Peacemaker with him this time.

"He might just be wearing a gun he managed to put his hands on."

"Well, that description matches a lot of men, but I haven't seen any strangers around here in the past few days."

"Well, I was tracking him and the men who broke him out. One of them told me he was headed here."

"Maybe you beat him."

Roper remembered Bill Tilghman saying the same thing to him the last time he'd tracked Sender, but this time he didn't think Sender was hiding in the cell blocks.

"Well, I'm going to take a look around town," Roper told him. "And I'll probably spend the night."

"Better spend a few days, if you're expecting him," Parnell said.

"You're probably right."

"Wanna get a steak later?"

"Add a beer and you got a deal."

"I'll meet you at Billy Joe's Café in two hours, down the street. Best steak in town. That should give you time to look around."

"Okay."

Roper headed for the door, then stopped and turned back.

"How's Tina?"

"McCord's woman? Still around. How did

that go anyway?"

"Turned out to be a mess, with a lot of dead people," Roper said.

"What was it all about?"

"I'll tell you later," Roper said, "over that steak."

Roper stopped at the livery to put up his palomino and make sure he got the right treatment. He also talked to the livery man about strangers in town.

"Ain't seen nobody looks like that," the old man said. "Fact is, you're the first stranger to stop here with a horse in a few days."

"Okay, thanks. I'd like to leave my rifle, saddle, and saddlebags here until I get a room. That okay?"

"Sure thing, mister. I ain't never seen a saddle like that, with a holster sewed to it."

"Comes in handy sometimes."

Roper started his walk around town. It was probably too much to hope for that he'd run into Sender on the street. He poked his head into some of the stores, the cafés, stopped in saloons to talk to bartenders. Nobody knew more than they did when it came to strangers in town.

In a little saloon called the Corral, a

bartender named Benny said, "I know John Sender."

"You know him?"

"Well," the man said, "I mean, I heard of him."

"You know him on sight?"

"I guess," Benny said. "I saw him a few years ago. Yeah, I guess I'd know him."

"And you haven't see him?"

"Not in Saint Joe."

"Well, I'm going to be staying in town. If you see him, find me or Sheriff Parnell as soon as possible."

"What hotel you gonna be in?"

"Recommend one."

"The Parker. Ain't the best, but it ain't the worst either."

"Sounds good. Thanks, Benny."

Roper left the Corral and walked to the Parker Hotel to get his room.

"What'd you find out today?" Parnell asked.

"Nothing," Roper said. "I walked around town, talked to some people, and came up empty. Sender's not in town."

"I told you that."

"I did find a bartender who knew him on sight," Roper said. "If he shows up, at least I have another pair of eyes."

"Who was that?"

"Benny, over at the Corral?"

"Ah, Benny."

"What's wrong with Benny?"

"I just wouldn't trust everything he says, Roper," Parnell said. "Just be careful around him."

"Yeah, okay, I will."

Their steaks came and Roper discovered Parnell was right. The steak was excellent.

"You were gonna tell me about your case," Parnell reminded him. "What was his name?"

"Westover."

"Yeah, that one."

"Not my finest hour," Roper said. "I should have stayed away from that one. They were lying to me from the start."

"About what?"

Roper really hadn't discussed the case with anyone since he'd gotten back to Denver. He didn't have any friends in town that he had those kinds of discussions with. He had some close friends around the country, but hadn't seen any of them in some time. Maybe this was the time to talk it over with a lawman.

"Westover and his 'friends,' " he started, "McCord, Quinn, Wilkins, Hampstead, and Templeton, were separated from their unit. It was near the end of the war. In fact, this incident might have taken place after Lee surrendered." Roper was telling Parnell things he'd read in the file Lieutenant Prince had given him.

"They came across a group of Confederate soldiers in a similar situation, but these soldiers had something with them. They had a wagonload of gold bars they'd apparently stolen from the Union. Well, there was a skirmish, Westover and his men won. They killed all the Johnny Rebs and recovered the gold."

"And got a medal for it?"

"Well, only Westover got the Medal of Honor because he was the ranking soldier."

"So the others were mad they didn't get a medal?" Parnell asked. "That's what it was all about?"

"Not quite," Roper said. "The United States government decided that only half the missing gold was recovered."

"Decided?"

"Decided, claimed, whatever," Roper said. "Anyway, they suspected that Westover and his buddies hid half the gold and recovered it after the war."

"Did they?"

"I don't know," Roper said. "They're all dead. If they did, and they each got away with a share, they sure did different things with it. Westover — or his wife — parlayed his into a fortune. The others seemed to have wasted it. Except for McCord."

"Why McCord?"

"Well, you said he was killed soon after he got back from the war," Roper said. "I'm assuming he didn't have time to spend his share. In fact . . ." Roper paused as something occurred to him.

"In fact, what?"

"When I was here last time and you took me to see Tina, I noticed she had good furniture in her house. Old, but good. And the same with her rifle. Somebody — her or Vince McCord — bought that stuff when they had money."

"And you think the money came from the gold?" Parnell asked.

"Maybe he kept the gold behind for her."

"Does she look like she had a fortune in gold?"

"If she did, it looks like she spent it well," Roper said.

"It looks to me like she didn't spend it at all."

"Or spent it smartly, so that people wouldn't know."

Parnell frowned, then asked, "Do you think she'd have any of it left?"

"I don't know," Roper said. "I don't really

365

know how much they each got."

"Or if they got any," Parnell said. "You don't know for sure, do you?"

"Well, they fell out over something," Roper said. "What, if not gold?"

"You know," Parnell said, "after the bank robbery that got McCord killed, they never did recover that twenty thousand."

"So you're thinking Tina had the money?"

"Makes as much sense to me as her having the gold."

"Maybe," Roper said, "we should go and ask her."

Just as last time Tina greeted them at the door with her rifle.

"Whatcha want?" she demanded.

"Tina, remember me?" Roper asked. "A couple of months ago maybe?"

She didn't answer.

"Twenty dollars?"

"Oh, yeah," she said, lowering the rifle. "Come on in."

Roper and Parnell approached the house as Tina turned and walked inside. As they entered, she was putting on a pot of coffee.

"Tina," Roper said, "I want to ask you about the gold."

Parnell looked shocked at Roper's bluntness, but the detective didn't want to beat around the bush. He still had John Sender to find.

She turned to look at him and asked, "What gold?"

"The gold Vince came home with from the war."

She stared at Roper for a few seconds, then turned back to the stove.

"Siddown," she said. "I'll bring the coffee."

Roper and Parnell sat at the table and waited. Tina came over with three mugs of coffee. She set one carefully in front of each of them, and then sat down across the table.

"Vince came back from the war with gold," she said. "Ill-gotten gold. And then he got killed."

"And what happened to the gold?"

"I buried it."

"Where?" Parnell asked.

"With him," she said.

"What?"

"It's in his coffin?" Roper asked.

She nodded.

"Why?"

"I told you," she said. "It was ill-gotten."

"Tina, what bought this furniture, and that rifle?" Roper asked.

"Vince bought it all, before he died. After that I never touched any of the money, or the gold."

"I find that hard to believe, Tina," Parnell said.

"I don't," Roper said. "Look around you."

"Then what have you been livin' on, Tina?" Parnell asked. "The twenty thousand?"

Tina looked away.

"Wait a minute," Roper said. "McCord's gold was ill-gotten gains, but not the twenty thousand that came from the bank?"

"These people," she said, "the fine townspeople, my neighbors, they looked down on me for years. Why should I worry about their money?"

"Must be almost gone by now, though," Roper said. "After all, twenty thousand can't last forever."

"I was careful," she said, "spent no more than a thousand a year. But yeah, it's gone."

Parnell sat back in his chair, looked at Roper.

"How much gold is in the coffin, Tina?" Roper asked.

"I don't know," she said. "Most of Vince's share."

"And you've never dug any of it up?"

"No," she said, squirming. "I thought about it, but I can't go into a cemetery and dig up a grave."

Roper wondered if, given more time, she might have gotten brave enough. But now it was too late.

"Okay, Tina," Roper said. "Thanks."

He and Parnell walked outside and headed back to town.

"There's gold in Vince McCord's grave," Parnell said. "Are we just gonna leave it there?"

"No," Roper said. "We'll dig it up."

"And what? Give it back to the government?"

"I think the people of this town deserve the money more than the government does," Roper said. "And you'll be a hero for recovering the bank's money so many years later. Make the local police department look bad."

"Or," Parnell said, "we could dig it up and split it."

"Why do I think," Roper asked, "that you're too much of a lawman to be serious?"

While Parnell was making arrangements to have some men dig up the grave, Roper waited outside the sheriff's office, seated in a straight-backed wooden chair. While he sat, he saw a man come riding down the street on a gray horse. The silver from his pistol reflected the sun.

John Sender.

Roper got up from his chair and said to himself, "Let's hope the third time is the charm."

to him if you want."

"I'd appreciate that."

Sheriff Parnell got up and said, "Come on."

They stepped outside, and Roper said, "My horse is at the livery."

"You won't need your horse. We can walk."

As he followed the sheriff until he got an uncomfortable feeling about where they were headed.

Roper had been able to tell himself earlier that the lawman was walking him to boot him just outside of town. Now he looked down at the badge, at the holstered gun, and simply said, "Tell me about it."

"What happened?"

"He and his boys got drunk one day and decided they'd like to rob my bank."

"We got that during it."

"No, sir," Parnell said. "They robbed the bank, all right, killed two tellers, one of 'em was a woman. They got away with over twenty thousand."

"So what happened?"

"Posse tracked 'em down, brought 'em back, and hanged 'em in the center of town. No trial."

Roper rode back to town without Hartwick, who stayed behind to discuss the paperwork with Victoria. When he got to town, he returned his horse to the stable, then walked to the nearest bank. He deposited the check Victoria had given him for his fee and an advance on expenses, arranged to have the money transferred to his own bank, and walked out with some cash in his pocket. After that he went back to his hotel to work out a schedule for himself. The men whose names Victoria had given him all lived in points west, so he was going to have to map out a plan of action.

Victoria's handwriting was very flowery, but he could make it out well enough:

Vincent McCord, Saint Joseph, Missouri
Gerald Quinn, Vega, Texas
Henry Wilkins, Jerome, Arizona